Yvonne Vera

THE STONE VIRGINS

YVONNE VERA is one of Zimbabwe's most acclaimed writers and social critics. She was born in Bulawayo, where she is now director of the National Gallery, and is the author of *Butterfly Burning* (FSG, 2000) and *Without a Name* and *Under the Tongue* (FSG, 2002). The recipient of numerous international accolades, Vera has been awarded the 1997 Commonwealth Writers Prize (Africa Region) for *Under the Tongue*, the 2002 Berlin Literature Prize (work in translation) for *Butterfly Burning*, and the 2002 Macmillan (UK) Writer's Prize for Africa (adult fiction) for *The Stone Virgins*. In 2003, she won Italy's Feronia Prize for *Butterfly Burning* and was a Hurston/Wright Legacy Award nominee for *Without a Name* and *Under the Tongue*.

THE STONE VIRGINS

THE STONE VIRGINS

Yvonne Vera

Farrar, Straus and Giroux

New York

To John H. C. Jose
For your essential and remarkable qualities,
travels and earth harmonies

Farrar, Straus and Giroux
18 West 18th Street, New York 10011

Printed in the United States of America
Originally published in 2002 by Weaver Press, Zimbabwe
Published in 2002 in the United States by Farrar, Straus and Giroux
First American paperback edition, 2003

The Library of Congress has cataloged the hardcover edition as follows:
Vera, Yvonne.
   The stone virgins / Yvonne Vera.
     p. cm.
   ISBN-13: 978-0-374-27008-7 (hc : alk. paper)
   ISBN-10: 0-374-27008-2 (hc : alk. paper)
   1. Sisters—Fiction. 2. Violence—Fiction.   3. City and town life—
Fiction.   4. Women—Zimbabwe—Fiction.   5. Zimbabwe—Fiction.
I. Title.

PR9390.9.V47 S76 2003
823'.914—dc21

                  2002025004

Paperback ISBN-13: 978-0-374-52894-2
Paperback ISBN-10: 0-374-52894-2

Designed by Jonathan D. Lippincott

www.fsgbooks.com

20 19 18 17 16 15 14 13 12

With gratitude to the city of Munich for residency at Villa Waldberta,
Feldafing, where this novel was completed.

1950–1980

Selborne Avenue in Bulawayo cuts from Fort Street (at Charter House), across to Jameson Road (of the Jameson Raid), through to Main Street, to Grey Street, to Abercorn Street, to Fife Street, to Rhodes Street, to Borrow Street, out into the lush Centenary Gardens with their fusion of dahlias, petunias, asters, red salvia, and mauve petrea bushes, onward to the National Museum, on the left side. On the right side, and directly opposite the museum, is a fountain, cooling the air; water flows out over the arms of two large mermaids. A plaque rests in front of the fountain on a raised platform, recalling those who died in the Wilson Patrol. Wilson Street. Farther down the road is a host of eucalyptus trees, redolent, their aroma euphoric. Selborne Avenue is a straight, unwavering road, proud of its magnificence. The first half, beginning at the center of the city, is covered with purple jacaranda blooms. Vibrant. These large trees stand high off the ground, with masses of tiny leaves; their roots bulge off the earth where they meet rock, climb over, then plunge under the ground. Wedged in between them are the flamboyant trees, with blistering red blooms, flat-topped, which take over territory from December to January, brightening the sky louder than any jacaranda could. The rest of the city is concrete and sandstone. Except here and there, a pride of cassias, flowering in resplendent yellow cones in June and July; then the temperature is at its lowest.

But first, the jacarandas. Their leaves and petals merge above the wide street and the pavements flanking it. The trees create a dazzling horizon. On the face of every passerby, the flickering movement of the leaves traces shadows of the trees like spilled dye, while light swims from above through their dizzying scent; the shadow is fragrant, penetrating. These trees, carefully positioned to color the road, create a deep festive haze. Bell-shaped petals carpet the street scene where a veiled bride and her maids suddenly appear from the magistrate's court at the Tredgold Building and drive a few blocks down to Centenary Park; they emerge out of polished cars in twirling gowns and fingers of white silk, clutching bouquets of pink carnations. They circle the fountain, and the groom. Their poses are measured and delicate. The groom wears a tailcoat, a pleated shirt, a gray cummerbund, and a single white buttonhole rose. The photographer bends and shifts and shields his lens from glare, from spray, but not from the blooms. From the beginning of October come a relentless heat and a gushing rain; November beats the petals down. The heat is intense. Long after the blooms have withered, the small leaves turn yellow and then dry. They rain down. The trees now are naked and majestic, while feathery seeds waft into the glassy sky. They drift. Higher than the trees. They land in the sky.

Selborne is the most splendid street in Bulawayo, and you can look down it for miles and miles, with your eyes encountering everything plus blooms; all the way from the laced balcony of Sir Willoughby's Douslin House (he was among the first pioneers with the British South African Company), or from the Selborne Hotel (built 1897) adjacent to it, or even from Thomas Meikle's Department Store. Selborne takes you to the Ascot Shopping Centre and Ascot Racecourse, where the horses bristle and canter past the Matsheumhlophe River, out of the city limits to the neat suburbs of Riverside, Hillside, Burnside. On your way to one of these fine suburbs, you may choose to turn into Catherine Berry Drive, or Phillips Way, which brings you past the Bulawayo City Golf Club green, to the smaller streets, secluded. Named after English poets— Kipling, Tennyson, Byron, Keats, and Coleridge. Before all that, Selborne Avenue is straight and unbending; it offers a single solid view, undisturbed.

Selborne carries you straight out of the city limits and heads all the way to Johannesburg like an umbilical cord; therefore, part of that city is here. Its joy and notorious radiance are measured in the sleek gestures of city laborers, black, who voyage back and forth between Bulawayo and Johannesburg and hold that city up like a beacon; when they return home, they are quick of step and quick of voice. They have learned something more of surprise, of the unexpected: of chance. They have been dipped deep in the gold mines, helmeted, torchlit, plummeted, digging for that precious gold which is not theirs. Not at all. They are not only black; they are outsiders. They make no claim. This is paid work, so they do it. Egoli . . . they say and sigh . . . about Johannesburg. The way they pronounce the name of that city, say it, fold it over the tongue, tells you everything; you can see the scaffolding and smell frangipani at nighttime, in Jo'burg. They are nostalgic and harbor a self-satisfied weariness that belongs to those who pursue divine wishes, who possess the sort of patience required to graft lemon trees and orange trees and make a new and sour crop.

They are content. They know how to evade gazes. They can challenge the speculative, the hostile and suspicious inquiries about their presence in the city, and this without flicking an eyelid. They click their fingers, move one knee forward, and dance mightily. To begin with, only their fingers move, tap-dance heel to toe, with a body as free as a weed in running streams. What they touch, they sing of with scorn; what they scorn, they do not touch.

Their trousers hang low past their heels, loose, baggy, and their hands tuck into large pockets and beat over their thighs in a quick motion. These men are impatient, ready to depart. They are uneasy, almost ready to return to Jo'burg empty-handed, to work there with appetite, with that steady easy zeal which accompanies anything temporary. Ready to sleep under the most luminous streetlights, to find places where they can bury their hurt and make love to new women while the sound of pennywhistles and bicycle tires sliding on tar urges them on. And anonymity.

Home is Bulawayo. This side of the city, not the other, their own side separated. Over and past Lobengula Street, the last road before you touch Fort Street and penetrate the city, before this, beyond. When they return here, neighbors give way and let them pass, and they enjoy suddenly being regarded as strangers in their own town, where everyone listens intently to their sun-dried whispers, examines their indolence and scorn, respects their well-decorated idleness, their cobra-skin belts and elephant-skin hats, eloquent, topped with their exciting layabout tones, why not, what with their cross-belts pulling their waistlines up when it suits them, on an afternoon when they attend soccer matches at Barbourfields Stadium, or Luveve Stadium, or White City Stadium. There they watch a game between Highlanders and any visiting team, whatever its name. So they put on their expensive shirts, which they fold carelessly up to the elbow, and their Slim Jim ties dangle all the way to the waist. What is more, they know some gum-boot dance, some knuckle-ready sound, some click song.

Their readiness is buoyed by something physical, their portable radios, their double-doored wardrobes, recently purchased, which they squeeze into small single rooms with low roofs, already tight and bursting with metal single beds, paraffin stoves, and display cabinets lined with silk flowers, teapots, breakable plates. Bright, colorful carpets from Nield Lukan to cover the cold township cement. No anxiety, even though in a week or less these new carpets will be choked with dust, and they have available to them nothing more than grass brooms, with which they will raise the dust off them, and let it settle, and raise it again. Midday. The men change into their double-vent jackets and their bright scarves, and walk easily down the street. Heat or rain. On Selborne.

In a secluded bar, black men recite all they can remember about that time when Satchmo was suddenly in their midst, taking their song, their song, "Skokiaan," from their mouths and letting it course through his veins like blood, their blood. The wonder of it. The enduring wonder of it. The love of it. The Bulawayo men play it again in their half-lit bars, wondering if their memory is true, if indeed they have touched the arm and sleeve of that glorious man, that Satchmo. The basement. A dark dank room in one of the finest hotels on Selborne Avenue, a storage place for empty beer bottles and crates and disused cutlery, where only the black workers descend; they note the amusement and let it be, from midnight till dawn.

Dream begets dream. Smoke burns on an evening and buries talk and blinds the view. The drinking glasses passing from hand to hand are improvised from brown Castle beer bottles cut in the middle. Drinks spill over the tray and are cuddled between elbow and breast. They clink and splash between the lowest chairs and the highest chairs and among the blossoming yellow shadows cast by the kerosene lamps pegged to the walls, where they hang, swing, hang. Nothing is permanent, neither anger nor caress, just swinging. In that half dark, elbows, handshakes, and knees quiver and navigate all the way to the back of the room, slip and settle down, while pledges and promises spoil and are reversed, as short-lived as the moth wings squashed under their feet. Someone curses. The insult is brief, is lost, as someone else whistles a friendly tune that lasts. A glass drops and breaks. The floor is wet and slippery as the beer dissolves into dirt and cement and the fragments of glass. The eyes numb and burning with smoke, the humming voices, the quiet afterward, as though anything could silence despair and turn it into a private matter. They speak low, in tones docile and easy. Inebriated; the night, the smoke, the music beating their soles.

A woman tugs a short skirt downward to cover her knees. Her panty hose is laddered nylon all the way to the heels, but who is checking in this kind of half dark, half love; she just wants the feeling of panty hose, if nothing else. She moves her waist, and the nylon stretches from her waist all the way to her toes. A round wooden table is held still by a folded newspaper tucked beneath one of its four unstable legs; the top is worn smooth by friction from naked arms. A man rests his folded arms on the table. His fingers taper down, his hands slack; the floor is near. His gaze on this woman, on this skirt, and these knees, is solid. He says nothing. He wants nothing. He lets her be. If she can, she will love him come what may. Every night, he has been here, watching. When he is not here, he is thinking about being here. Every subtle difference in the room interests him, the movement of each chair, the betrayals, the voices intertwined, the smoke circling the knees. He takes a sip from the perfume rising from this woman's elbows. He moves his chair close. Real close. She notes his movement and adjusts her gaze. She slides one leg above another. Her right. She looks smoothly down, under the table. Her toe is touching his knee. She presses her naked elbow firmly on the tabletop, as near and detached as she can be. She slides one hand into the warm cleft of her arm. An elbow bent.

The band has been playing softly on the raised platform in a corner of the room. The bandleader sits back in his pale blue shirt and his navy blue trousers and his sky blue tie, and in his deep blue voice softly says, "Did you say Louis . . . Louis Armstrong? . . . " He rises. He plays a trumpet. Plays his "Skokiaan" with Louis before his eyes, as far as he can imagine to the left, under that dimming lamp and the smell of kerosene light. And everyone agrees that yes, he played with Louis; there is no doubt about that. He is Satchmo—so what, can he play upstairs in the President's Room? The country is landlocked, bursting. The war is in their midst. The Umtali-Beira railway line has been bombed. He sure cannot play upstairs, but it is clear he is trying to get that train where it is heading; he is crossing that line, and his trumpet is glittering in the faint light, his eyes squeezed blind.

They want him to be heard above ground—somewhere. This is the day they are all waiting for. Not for Satchmo to come, and go, and play their "Skokiaan," leaving them breathless and blue, but for this man to carry their own desires above ground—somewhere. Not to cover their sorrow with their hats, like that, their trumpet covered with a hat, like that. To be honest, there is nothing they actually wish to enjoy up there, not all that velvet on the chairs, all that ribbon on the curtain, and all that frill on all that curtain . . . They have no wish to acquire that. All they want is to come and go as they please. At independence, they just want to go in there, and leave, as they please, not to sneak or peep, but to come, and go, as they please. They would stay gone if they could establish this one condition, to come and go, as they please. Satchmo.

The city is built on a grid. Where Selborne meets Main Street, the building there forms a sharp turn; the same angle is repeated over and over again, street to street, all the way down Selborne to Ascot Centre, the tallest building as far as the eye can see. A man in an orange overall sweeps the corner along Main Street, at Douslin House. He has a stubborn zeal, rapid strokes that pull the street dirt of bottle tops, plastic containers, paper, fruit peels all toward him till he forms a small pile, and then he bends, scoops it with bare hands, rises, empties it into a wheeled plastic bin beside him. His lips are moving. His arms are swinging. He pauses. He looks around him for any stray paper, as though he is seeking a stray thought and finds none. He looks again, stepping aside, from toe to shoulder, moving his silent lips. He wipes his eyebrows, only his eyebrows, with the tips of his right fingers. He brings the fingers down to the long handle of his broom. The handle leans on his left shoulder. He stands still. His body mute.

Only his fingers are moving. Tapping. Quietly. On the broom. Lovingly. The cars drive past. One by one. They drive quickly past. He moves away as though from his own shadow, steps from the tarmac onto the pavement. He is now on elevated ground under the raised balcony, close to the wall of the building, no longer completely on Main Street, not quite on Selborne, either. Standing here, at this corner, his body is softly disturbed.

The city revolves in sharp edges; roads cut at right angles. At noon, shadows are sharp and elongated. Streets are wide. Widest at intersections. In this city, the edge of a building is a profile, a corner . . . *ekoneni.* The word is pronounced with pursed lips and lyrical minds, with arms pulsing, with a memory begging for time. *Ekoneni,* they say, begging for ease, for understanding.

The corner of a building is felt with the fingers, rough, chipped cement. You approach a corner; you make a turn. This movement defines the body, shapes it in a sudden and miraculous way. Anything could be round the corner. A turn, and your vision sees new light; nothing is obscured. You are as tall as these buildings sprouting from the ground. You are as present as time, solid and whole; the heart beating is your own, the breath warming your lips as alive as this moment, as true and unhurried. *Ekoneni.* A vista, and Selborne Avenue is stretching from your forehead all the way to the stars. Your fear floats to the skin, like touch.

Ekoneni is a rendezvous, a place to meet. You cannot meet inside any of the buildings because this city is divided; entry is forbidden to black men and women; you meet outside buildings, not at doorways, entries, foyers, not beneath arched windows, not under graceful colonnades, balustrades, and cornices, but *ekoneni.* Here, you linger, ambivalent, permanent as time. You are in transit. The corner is a camouflage, a place of instancy and style; a place of protest. *Ekoneni* is also a dangerous place, where knives emerge as suddenly as lightning. Death can be quick and easy as purses and handbags are snatched, discarded, and pockets are emptied. Tomorrow is near and forgotten.

Noon. A man wears his hat low, a cap squeezed down and shifted over the right eye. His faded and tight jacket, worn out at the elbow, is pulled down on one side by something heavy in the pocket, a flashlight, a folded umbrella, or something only he knows. His companion is swinging his head back and forth in quick rhythm; his fingers are held between his folded knees; his fingers are snapping—this is how certain truths are born, between thumb and forefinger. This sound alone ignites a hope larger than gloom.

The man with the cap falling over his nose turns his head round the corner and searches the distance. The lower part of his shirt collar is a sharp triangle pointing sideways; the edge of the collar is torn. He kicks the wall playfully with a well-worn shoe, quick, fast, eager. He is testing his own strength. He pulls back. He turns his back to the wall and leans back. He fumbles inside his jacket pocket, and brings out the stem of a bicycle pump, and raises it to his parted lips. First, he brushes his lips with the back of his hand, from wrist to thumb to forefinger. He curls down, his shoulders off the wall now. He blows into the folds of his fingers as though blowing into bone; a crystal sound follows his body as he slides downward on the edge of the building, feeling lighter. He hugs the ground with a frail body. His jacket is a heap on the cement. A handheld sound lengthens from the tip of his shoe, like a shadow. His companion has vanished.

Ekoneni. Here, love soars or perishes when lovers meet. The purpose of this encounter is to establish which of the two lovers is the survivor, which the quiet mind—which one is imbued with disasters, which is the channel of forgiveness, which one is the accuser, the architect of guilt.

The man stands on one edge of the building; meanwhile, on the other side, along the sharp dividing end of the wall, separate, the woman is waiting, too. Each of their elbows rests against the wall; their fingers search, uncertain, and curl over the wall, touch, without joining hands. When it suits them both, they will maneuver, move away in slow motion, their minds solitary. Or one of them turns completely round the corner to meet the other, soon, before he or she moves away and disappears. Her hand moves slowly up his arm and holds him tight. As though mutually agreed they proceed together, two shadows. Often, they choose to maintain territory, *ekoneni.* Just waiting, knowing full well someone is on the other side, waiting also. A leg rises up the wall and glides down. The shoulder leans farther back. The heel rubs against the wall. Then, as though responding to a sudden whistle, the woman and the man both move away and go in separate directions. They wander off without remorse, into the distance. They have postponed surrender and yielded to the temptation of delays. They leave no trace of their presence. Not here. Something else materializes, another quick agony, perhaps a song handheld, gracefully, like desire.

Lovers part again and again. They move on, holding their heads high, as though they have never met, as though they can each command the movement of the sun, yet each feels the other's absence. When it reaches the earlobe, a word is soft like skin.

For them to part, it must be something he did not say, something she did not say; it could not be anything either of them said, not with the scent he feels fading along his naked arm, her warm breath, remembered. No. Their fingers have touched. For them to part, it must be the unsaid words between them, the fear of finding out that what has not been said would remain so, long after everything else has been said. The silence parts them, but they remember, their voices foraging.

What was that he said to her about having a photograph taken at the African Photo Studio on Lobengula Street and Eleventh Avenue? She wants to go to Kay's Photo Studio on Jameson Street, where they give you a small mirror for one hand and a wineglass for the other while the camera clicks and flashes and another self flickers right past you while you stand still, and time stands still, and the self that you have prepared all week and now set free falls into the palm of your hand as easy as morning. Your finger is curled tight over the slim, long stem of the glittering glass, your eyebrows are pencil sharp, and the smile you have prepared in the mirror hanging behind the door is not all tucked right at the edges, almost not there, but your head is as far back on your shoulders as it could ever be. You are looking just fine; the city is part of you and you are not part of the city. A lift of your arm captures its mood.

At Star Photo Studio, just across the street from Kay's, they make you sit on a high stool with your back to the camera and ask you to hold the mirror as high as your shoulder, then turn your head slowly back till the photographer says to stop, and you do, and hold your neck still, or something like that. Two selves emerge out of every picture, so you get your money's worth, for sure. A backdrop of sailing ships shows that you are not as landlocked in this city as everywhere else in the country. She wants to see that sailing ship and that wide expanse of sea where her own body would fit and float and she would be as far from herself as she ever could be, as well traveled as the camera confirms. She is not sure because she has not been to Star Photo Studio yet. But she will be. If not with him, with someone else. They part too completely, knowing only this.

What they both know fully by heart are contradictions. They both recall lost chances like warm fires—with fondness. They nurture risks like tenderness; they love uncertainties the way they love the drumming of a brief rain on zinc roofs, the way they love the pale silence after church bells. They love the vanishing quality of things: a woman breathless.

They love their own voices dreaming, their own fingers dreaming on each other's bodies. They love memory reaching out, veined as arms. They avoid ladders, stairs, pillars; when they can, they stay on level ground.

Hats are borne on drifting laughters, then captured below the hemline, under the billowing skirts of the women—hats tossed like feathers, like sentiments. The day is too short, as brief as the turn of a man's hat falling on bare arms.

They leave the city, here, where a woman lingers at a corner of the street, her arms heavy with a basket of pomegranates; a cloth is tied over the slippery handle of her basket. She stands, with the basket at her feet, her brow tightened, remembering an unpleasant encounter perhaps, wondering what she forgot to remember, if anything. She beats her gathered skirts as though shaking off grains of sand, while a stream of people hurry to Lobengula Street and pass by without casting a single glance at her. When she is ready, she hugs the basket back to her waist and hurries, too, toward Lobengula Street; the incessant voices, the jostling bodies amid the tomatoes spilling in mounds onto the pavement, the smell of guava fruit, all mingling with the sound of braking wheels. "*Tshova! Tshova!*" Voices explode and bodies scramble into the overloaded vehicle, which speeds quickly out of the city.

If you turn from Selborne Avenue into Grey Street and go west, you can drive all the way out, without turning either left or right, to the ancient Matopo Hills, those tumbling rocks reaching out to the lands of Gulati, past that to Kezi. Kezi: two hundred kilometers from the bustling porch of the Selborne Hotel, where parasols mingle with disgruntled miners, bankers, and day-to-day merchants, where industry is brisk. Here the delivery boy, with telegrams and the day's post, waits outside before someone finds him and relieves him of the mail.

K ezi is a rural enclave. Near it are the hills of Gulati. When you leave Kezi, you depart from the most arable stretch of flatland there is. There are towering boulders of rock, then hills and an undulating silence for a whole bus journey, till on the horizon you see Bulawayo beckoning. If at night, city lights glow like a portion of the sky.

The Bulawayo-Kezi road leads finally to Thandabantu Store before the bus heads back to the city. Beyond Thandabantu Store, the huts spread evenly on each side of the dirt road, their grass roofs so low that they sag, spread, and fall over the mud walls. Almost touching the ground, the roofs create circles of cool earth close to the mud walls and the rectangular entrances. The walls appear reduced in height, shortened by the thatch and the shadows beneath. The huts are flattened and, from a distance, form perfect circles of calm merged with the land, though often finger-painted designs mark the surface closest to the ground. When it rains, water settles briefly on the grass, not running off smoothly or quickly. After the rain, the top layer of wet, partly decomposed thatch is the softest scent of living things there is—it is life itself. Tall dry grass stands between the sparse trees, as brown as the soil and as still as the heated air, the abundant silence. There are tumbling rocks resting between the trees, sliding along the sides of the small hills.

In another distance, trees grow wildly at the bottom of a large flat boulder, crouched, whose back rises into the sky; the land here is rock. Under the large rocks, there is water. Meanwhile, a tree extends its branches over an expanse of rock. The tree clings, and curls underneath with roots; large, wide, plastered against the smooth surface, the roots are as hard as stone; each is a gleaming gray, peeling, firm. And everywhere there are thornbushes.

Within this view of the huts emerge narrow, meandering footpaths leading in and out of every homestead, to the river, to the road. Elongated boulders of granite perched on flat ground rise among the sedate huts that stretch into wider settlements separated only by vast clearances of cultivated fields, and an unending canopy of daylight. Breaking the pattern are a few brick buildings, which can be seen throughout— scattered, permanent structures with asbestos roofs. The land dips briefly into a small valley, farther down, away from the fields; the trees here are higher. In the far distance but clearly visible to the eye are the lands of Gulati, whose hills shape the entire eastern horizon. Even from this distance, these are the greatest heights, soaring above any of the hills or rocks of Kezi, swallowing the earth around them, beckoning. Each morning, the sun climbs softly from behind those hills and casts a furtive glow. It is full light before the complete shape of the sun appears above the towering hills of Gulati, at midday it is directly overhead, and then finally it sets properly on flat ground, where land meets sky, in Kezi, opposite the immense horizon of stone hills. At night, this difference is visible: on one side, the stars vanish suddenly into the density of the heavy rocks, now a quiet and impenetrable mass of darkness; on the other side, the sensation is that of walking directly on the stars. So near and infinite is the sky that the mind floats, imbued with the most enigmatic sight. Darkness is fluid, the sky and land inseparable.

Thandabantu Store is suspended just off the edge of the busy and winding Kezi-Bulawayo road, where the ground dips unexpectedly, then flattens, located right where the road rises steeply and determinedly from the narrow bridge over the Kwakhe River, now dry. In truth, the bus drives from Bulawayo to Kezi, then back to Bulawayo. But on the slim wooden plaque suspended next to the conductor's window, Kezi comes first, and in the minds of the residents of Kezi, of course, Kezi comes first: the bus, therefore, is seen as driving from Kezi to Bulawayo to Kezi, over and over again during the entire week. Some of the population has been to Bulawayo, and people go back and forth as they please. Some dream of nothing but Bulawayo; some seldom think of leaving Kezi.

Whenever the Kwakhe River is full, the bus fails to cross the bridge; it lags, and people have to spend a day and maybe half a night waiting on the other side, nestling their treasured wares gathered from the city, while listening to the river sulk. The bridge becomes covered entirely, as if it had never been there. The river always subsides quickly no matter how full, the water chasing the rocks, then disappearing farther down, released into the earth, sinking—that retreating part of the riverbed is a mystery—the soil sucks the water down. The river suddenly wanes and loses its curves; it is slim, narrow. The remaining water trickles outward to pour into the wider and more resilient Nyandu River, way past Umthetho, that tranquil granite rock in the distance, large, where old men go to recline, and die, in silence. For a long time, there has not been enough rain to bury the bridge; the rain is sporadic, apologetic. The river has been so burned by the sun you can measure it grain by glittering grain, and by the number of children swarming on it like bees.

Young boys run through the soft soil with their naked feet cushioned; the soil slides a warm touch between their toes and they leap into one another's arms, their joy, their voices swell to the river's smooth and naked bank. This same soil is littered with empty packets of Willard potato chips—onion-flavored, vinegared, salted. Then broken bottles of Coca-Cola, sharp and dangerous, empty red one-liter cartons of Chibuku beer. The smell of urine emanates from every nearby rock. The children take empty plastic bags from O.K. Bazaars, brought from Bulawayo, stuff them with newspapers, shape them into firm sizable balls, and scream with delight each time they kick not only the plastic ball but clouds of pink Kwakhe River dust higher than their own shoulders, higher than the caps on their foreheads, which they have just received from Toppers Stores.

The caps have been distributed to them free of charge by the tall woman who arrives from the city in a brightly colored van. She wears a red pencil skirt, high heels that sink into the river soil, so she has to lean forward to walk, and sunglasses so dark that they never get to see her eyes. She deposits khaki uniforms for boys six to fourteen at the store—for sale. She also leaves ties bearing the Toppers Stores label. The clothes rest on metal hangers held on hooks attached to the walls. The folds on them persist, pleats across the sleeves, stiff with extra starch. The boys consider these shirts with scorn, and a mild curiosity.

The van drives off in a cloud, and the boys chase after it anyway, for no reason at all, just to show they are neither quiet nor defeated, neither humble nor ignorant, not passive, but full of energy and might, not children either, but voiced presences with a will, with legs that can carry them in any direction they please, with instinct and jovial command, so they run in their longest strides, tumbling downward right down to the bridge, and watch the van sink and rise faster than even their own senses can recall, then gather a speed and turbulence that swallows them whole. And they wave. And stand. Puzzled. And drop their caps. And pick them up from the dust.

The boys tidy their minds and rub the dust off their noses, and sniff the air for its odor and surprise. Then they sit down on the edge of the dry river with Madeleine razors held tightly between their fingers and sharpen their pencils, rapidly spreading fine lead onto their knees. Sometimes the sharp blade of the razor slips, grazing a finger and slivering the skin off, and the boys, brave, choose to ignore that minor hurt and proceed, instead, to write at the back of their torn notebooks whatever comes easily to the mind, such as descriptions of the large pale green telephone booth that has just been installed but has no handset yet.

The green telephone booth. It can hold two people, standing, hidden from the stars, that is obvious. So in the night, lovers meet and whisper messages to each other, and pretend there is a vast distance between them, when in fact all there is to separate their bodies is nothing more traceable than a whisper, and much less substantial than darkness. Here, in what exists of this hopeful machine, they insert disused Rhodesian coins, copper pennies and silver shillings, and try different voices, which they whisper close to each other's ears—an angry pitch and nuance when they call for Ian Smith or call Geneva and Lord so-and-so, a sedate tone for their inner escapades.

Their voices more temporary than the darkness, they swing toward each other, having first retrieved their halfpennies, to secure touch, their knees holding, their lips tender, moving toward each other in order to ponder their proximity, to match their own voices, in synchrony, breathing in and out at the same pace, syllable for syllable, inhalation, pulse to pulse, wondering how long they can be this silent and this discreet, wondering if they can fulfill all those other promises that require daylight in order to be true, and instead offer each other what is easy and achievable, copies of Nick Carter novels and Agatha Christie stories. Novels the Kunene Mission School has confiscated and thrown out to the old women to use for their cooking fires, but which these hungry few have retrieved, salvaged, wanting to possess anything that is printed and can be read out around a fire, something that is not a birth certificate.

In this green booth, they hold hands where the handset should be, having sought the mouthpiece, the hearing piece, and found none. Having sought the telephone cord that would link them to the city center, with Bulawayo or even Salisbury, with Gwelo or Gatooma, and found none. Having sought the directory with all their names listed, and found none of their own, the one copy chained to the booth revealing the small printed names and addresses only of Bulawayo residents, people entirely unknown and uninteresting to them. Not Kezi, not their Kezi, just this tantalizing contraption left in their midst to mock their lack, to rouse their want.

The delay is part of the signature of their lives. This is familiar. Like the tarred road that ends abruptly at the Thandabantu Store and goes no farther, as though there were no possibility of the mind ever wanting to wander off steadily into the distance, farther than the eye can see. Indeed, as though it would never occur to the mind, to the body, to want simply to disappear from view. The road ends as though the builder ran out of materials and had no choice but to leave things exactly where they are, suspended, rough. The rest is dirt road going nowhere, for who knows what is right at the end of it, so narrow and tight that two cars cannot pass on it and each vehicle has to place one set of wheels on the road and let the other slide on the grass. The dust rises higher than the trees and boulders. When a car approaches from the opposite direction, you see the dust first, not the car. The car appears later, when the dust has settled and tomorrow has almost arrived.

They will have to wait months, maybe longer, for the telecommunications van to come again, all the way from Bulawayo, with its swaggering, young, newly trained black technicians in tight orange overalls, who suck at ice mints and spit into fires, their hair cut neatly, who speak in spurts because they have gone to mission schools like David Livingstone in Ntabazinduna. Their only fear is God; mankind they can deal with.

So elbows rest on top of the metal unit, which has digits carefully engraved on its buttons. This is unfinished business, clearly. Meanwhile, they collect telephone numbers belonging to factories and wholesale centers they have heard of— Blue Ribbon Foods and Security Mills and Archer Shirts, Kaufmann Shoes and Gees Refrigeration—all those places necessary to the city, but just workstations to the people in Kezi, places where one can locate long-lost uncles and relatives who have taken the Bulawayo bus all those many months ago and not come back, not written, not sent a message. They have faded into the city.

Now the store is hidden from view as though by a luminous, darkening wall; the colliding particles of dust dance, spread, and float out. The sun's rays move through it, and the dust glitters. The voices emerge from the bus, the laughter, the people calling to one another. The store emerges slowly as the orange filter settles, its edges and asbestos roof rising first like an outline drawn out of charcoal. Out of the dust upon which this edifice floats, the roof appears next, red, rippling to the front, where the figures on the veranda slowly rise as though wading out of water. The orange dust settles along the waists of the men, and the one man bending is buried from view, with only his raised arm visible, like a man drowning. The air forms a thick, blinding mist.

It is slow, this dust. It settles gradually once disturbed. The voices rise above the sound of the grinding bus wheels, above that heavy squeaking as the bus clambers up the bridge; then the store is suddenly present. The print on the facade reads clearly THANDABANTU STORE, large black letters on white paint. The radio from Thandabantu is louder than the voices emerging from the bus and calling for their goods to be brought down from the roof, where they have been tied down and have safely endured the long drive from the city. A shout for a discarded newspaper to be thrown through the window. A child crying for its mother stands under the wheels of the bus. A drunk man is awakened and told he has arrived in Kezi and must now disembark. He tumbles out, missing the last step as he drops out of the bus and leaps to the ground. He cries out, suddenly awake, for his purse is missing. This dust makes sound as slow as dream.

Thandabantu Store has a large wide veranda where often people meet and sit and talk and wait for the bus to arrive or any other traffic to go by, to stop, to deliver a message, a parcel, a plow, a human presence. They wait for nothing more than the lilt of their own voices.

A series of three steps, a foot apart and two meters wide, lead to a rectangular cement platform, the main floor of the veranda partly enclosed by a short brick wall. Two front pillars high enough to support the jutting zinc roof, painted red, which extends right across the full length of the store's front wall. This roof is lower than the primary asbestos roof above it, covering the main building, leaving a gap which carries some lettering. The enclosing walls of the veranda are about a meter from the ground and half as thick. Where they stop they create a comfortable flat surface wide enough to sit on.

The floor, once painted black, is now cracked, with chunks of cement missing and a rough grout exposed, its crevices slightly putrid with a mixture of spilled drinks and paraffin but the area is still usable, tolerable. There are hand-carved stools and abandoned Coca-Cola crates to sit on, a long metal bench, and the surrounding wall links pillar to pillar, its smooth and flat top a layer of cement. The veranda forms a partial shelter, an enclosure, a resting place.

Men sit along the wall with their legs hanging high off the ground; only the tips of their shoes touch the floor. They chat endlessly, knowingly, forgetfully. They sit with more confidence on the stools, their backs lowered and near the ground, leaning against the front wall of the store, near the doorway, their feet firm and anchored. Clouds of cattle pass by with bells beating under their necks, pausing to look around, then moving downward through the bridge to cross the Kwakhe River. A few meters away from Thandabantu Store are the hoofprints, the smell of dung, the sun, vermilion.

The store consists of one large room with high walls. Many shelves are located behind the counter, piled with Gold Star white sugar, tins of red fruit jam, and tins of condensed milk. The dust forms layers over the plastic bottles of Roil and Olivine and sunflower oil; no one bothers to keep them clean, not even the storekeeper, Mahlathini. And bags of sugar beans weigh down the shelves. There are posters everywhere on the walls, about life and Coca-Cola, malaria tablets, and Nespray milk.

In front of the store, close to the large marula tree, which stands higher than the roof of Thandabantu Store and higher than any other tree near or far, the impatient crowd rushes toward the bus to meet relatives and friends who have returned from the city, from Bulawayo. They find many; they find none. Each moment yields the fervent excitement of discovery. The bus, the bustle, is all under the tree—that is how tall the tree is, full of leaf and height, branches sweeping down over the bus, and enough marula fruit to accompany every leaf. The people push and shove endlessly, raise their voices high, shout through the opaque windows, searching, frantic. The conductor blows his whistle loud and long, and bodies reel and move away. The crowd falls back and lets the conductor swing the door open, outward. They surge forward once the passengers begin to spill out. Some are here to receive parcels that have been sent through the bus conductor, and so the people have to wait till he is ready to convey them or he calls out their names, and if he knows them and their names well, he calls out the names of their children also.

And letters from husbands, from lovers. And parcels of nylon stockings and skirts made of crushed silk, then red berets, then bangles. Bottles of Shield deodorant and Tomesei shampoo. And Ponds. And lip balm scented with lemon. Bubble gum that has a hint of cinnamon. Cocoa butter and plastic tubes of camphor cream. And a pouch full of divinely shaped buttons, so appealing in their smallness and multitude, the man just has to send them to his waiting woman to be kept somewhere, dusted regularly, kept free of moisture and termites, absolutely never to be used to repair any garment, but kept in Kezi. The woman slides her fingers into the pouch once in a while and feels the attractive polish of the buttons and their touch on her nails, sky blue, deep blue, full blue, and much bluer than anything blue, yet so transparent that she can see forever through them. He definitely will return on that Kezi-Bulawayo-Kezi bus. She will wait till he does or until he sends something else equally magnetic to restrain her impatience, something that he has discovered while rummaging in a corner of some room somewhere, or something he has found discarded on the desk of a white man who has hired him for some labor, some task; a man who, however, has too little time for this sort of misplaceable material treasure. This the black man takes without any fear of being discovered, and none of reprimand.

The bus also brings the disintegration of relationships, empty parcels with no letter enclosed, or a letter with a message of which the heart cannot partake, but always there are goods to be removed from the roof of the bus—mattresses, tables, chairs, blankets, pots, and sacks of maize seed to prepare for planting. To have brought a bed from the city, this is among the highest achievements. The goods are carefully lowered as arms reach, then carry the items down. Window frames for those who have started to build their houses with bricks. Metal door frames. A door with a metal handle, just like they have at Kunene Mission School. And even though water is still being carried all the way from the river or borehole by each and every household, a man not only brings a metal door frame; he also carries silver taps. Just in case.

The people disembark from the bus and go first into Thandabantu Store and buy whatever else it is they have forgotten to bring from Bulawayo, or whatever they identify, like, and can carry, or can fit into their many parcels. It is only after being at Thandabantu that they disperse into the village, feeling fortified and ready to deal with whatever uncertainty they left behind—an unresolved matter, an anxiety of their own—no matter how long or brief the time away. Even before the last dust from the bus wheels settles, they enter the store like fugitives. They enter into Thandabantu's welcoming veranda, chatting endlessly with the storekeeper, Mahlathini, greedily gathering details on who has died, who has married, whose cow has calved, who has moved from Gulati to settle in Kezi. They desire to know much more than this, much more than could ever be shaped into words. Truth is elusive; they settle for the evident; their own hearts, beating.

They are starving for the security of something they have left behind. Being absent witnesses, they seek knowledge about whatever it is that has happened in Kezi without their assistance. Thirsty, they plead deliverance from the rows of warm and dusty Fanta bottles that have sat on the shelves for weeks, untouched. They do not accept any change from the money they render, but sneer, proudly, tipping their hats at Mahlathini, composing some thought with which to linger purposefully at the counter, sliding one furtive hand into one neatly ironed trouser pocket as though to warm it, kneading a chin with an open palm, leaning both elbows on the greasy counter, asking and pondering the worth of each response. The year is just beginning, with its mixture of strong winds, full sun, and war.

They already miss and favor the city lights, whose brilliance ' outshines the moon; they miss the city's curse and caress, its movements, which are like an entire constellation, man-made. You can measure time in the city by its own particular scents and sounds—in the early morning, the smell of baking bread in the ovens at Lobels Bakery, spilled liquor fermenting in alleys, the dozens of wiry cats turning over the garbage bins and rummaging for food, the tumult of flower sellers outside the city hall at midday. Then, fuel and burning tar rise pungent from the fleet of cars, and penetrate every conversation, and late, late in the night, when the black people have vacated the city center except for the necessary few, the sight of white men at the Selborne Hotel as they gulp the clearest liquor from thumb-sized glasses, their faces a masquerade, their shoulders sunken with a baffling and private delight.

With boxes of Lobels choice assorted biscuits under their armpits, or lemon creams, or Mitchell's ginger biscuits, the disembarked squeeze into Thandabantu and buy bottles of Mazoe concentrated orange. They buy bread that has come from Bulawayo the same day, on the same Kezi-Bulawayo bus they have just vacated. There is always business for Thandabantu Store, and more than just money is passed around. As shelves empty, items are brought in from the back rooms in large cardboard boxes, and again various items are replaced in rows—baked beans, jam, soap. Coins clatter, voices thicken, and, through the window, the light outside begins to fade.

A man and a woman in matching sunglasses sit quietly under the marula tree and catch their breath. He wears a red shirt; she wears a red skirt. They have returned to the village, having gathered what they can about the city, about themselves. Ready, now, to wake to the smell of fires, to the cricket sounds and the white chorus of doves. They watch the bus, which has their hopes condensed all over its windows. Their clothes mingle in the same suitcase that is pinned down with black rubber bands onto the roof of the bus, dust filled, termite-free, ice cream stained. Folded neatly inside the suitcase, the embroidered white pillow covers they have shared in their city love and which they bought at Vidaya's that same day when they could not afford the twelve-by-twelve-inch plastic tray they had so wanted. It had one yellow rose on it, and no thorns.

People move close to the counter and fill the entire space and, as usual, refuse to budge. Their keen voices perforate every reality but their own. They whisper about the hills of Gulati, taking good care not to be heard, not to be identified with their own voices, leaving hardly a trace of their concealed agonies, except for the anger rising under their arms. They laugh. Close to their bodies is the city jive lingering along the ankle, where the turned-up hem of a trouser has now gathered a flour-fine layer of dust. Nothing betrays them as much as that unswinging arm with the choice assorted biscuits held tightly beneath, the clumsy handshake, and that single lonely hand sliding gently into the trouser pocket, seeking consolation, not warmth. To be in Kezi, to be in the bush, is to be at the mercy of misfortune: Fear makes their hearts pound like drums. The war so near, so close to the skin that you can smell it.

Thenjiwe walks across the road, joins the crowd, the goods, the searching voices. She holds the money for her purchases in a tight fist, a few coins in her right hand. She intends to buy a bottle of cooking oil, some flour, a packet of salt, a packet of tea, some matches. None of the faces or voices is familiar to her, so she moves on, raises one foot onto the first step, another, and suddenly her whole body is mingling with the excited voices spilling onto the floor beneath her feet. She must wait for an opportunity to enter the packed doorway filling with men's hats, and arms raised into triangles over their heads, while strong and protective palms slide over the grooved top of each hat, pressing the supple felt peak, holding down. Black, gray, and brown brims. The place is full. Thenjiwe is not in a hurry at all and can stand aside and absorb the melody, if not the dance.

A man sits alone at the edge of the stoop at Thandabantu Store; the shadow of the roof cuts his face into two halves, one dark, one light. Thenjiwe passes by. She notices him, then his silence. Thenjiwe pardons this man who drops his lashes when she approaches and lifts them as soon as he feels her shadow graze his knees. He moves his knees this way, that way. He rests his palms over his knees, spreading his fingers, swinging his knees till she turns her head and looks back, at his eyes and not his knees. At him. He feigns surprise and raises his eyebrows, asking a question, discovering if she needs some kind of help, offering abundant appeal.

She walks by and takes over the corner in his mind where some thought is trapped, some useless remembrance about fences with NO TRESPASS signs and NO WORK signs. A remembrance, of persecutions and possible agonies, of bold urgencies. Some hopeless memory hangs on a lone nail somewhere in his mind and disturbs him a little, makes him slightly frantic when he sits down, walks, or lifts an arm to complete one of three tasks, whichever task comes to mind, one at a time, and disturbs him slightly, like a wind fluttering, like that paper he once saw as a child as it floated on water in the Nyanyani River, the ink spilling off the words, the paper thinning, transparent, tearing, the words vanishing.

He leans his head toward her to catch whatever she might say in his regard, noting well the amusement breaking in her eyes. His knees no longer rocking, held down by her searching eyes. She stills his knees. He smiles a broad, even smile that has everything to do with her but nothing to do with his own past, his cautious memory, calm and hidden. Now something else in him is swinging, swinging, as she walks on by.

He is remembering. His eyes trace the motion of this memory. The whip raised high up, knotting the sky. The whip strikes ribbons of air behind her. He looks past her shoulders, way beyond. The cart is in the way, suspended between her and eternity. A horizon might save him; only the sky and earth could challenge her presence. The burnt evening sky coveting morning. The horizon sky. The cart tilting. Stopped. Where the bus has been. The dust rises into small clouds. He remembers this woman as though he has met her before, in some distance. It could only be her. But where? His voice opens beside her, breaking her stride, offering something that belongs to her. Something from himself. He has brought her a nameless gift. He is whistling amusement. He is amusement.

Now he pulls his knees back, his thumbs tucked under his armpits. He holds still and beats the ground with his foot, his foot raised and waiting, tapping away. He taps steadily on the cement floor. His own heart beating, he draws his foot closer to the metal can on which he sits, round its edge, and hooks the circle of its base with the back of his shoe, hugging her memory as she moves right past, and again his left foot draws forward, unable to be still, and he can hear the scratch of the tin, the hollow rhythm of sound from his foot beating his sole against hot metal. He holds still. The sun is setting.

She holds on, too cautious to turn her head, not this moment, but soon, past her own desire to look over the shoulder, to stop in front of him and say something, anything, to offer a single wholesome laugh, perhaps to raise him from his sitting position and bring him to her swaying height. Almost. Just to see who would touch the other first, who would extend a hand in greeting in the presence of so much uncertainty, so much harmony among strangers. His whistle is more than a confession—it is about himself, a whistle that, on the surface, has nothing to do with her, so self-involved, the sound of labor, of a man passing the time while he makes something useful, while he carves on wood, carves or just takes a turn round a wide street. Nothing musical or agonized, but not disinterested, either. She pulls in her own breath quietly while he continues to be preoccupied with the labor of his empty hands.

She forgives that and steps aside. Not disturbed, but disturbing. No longer wishing to escape. She is without shelter till he stops whistling amusement and leans on her, leans the full burden of his body on her, or so it seems.

She laughs to herself and kicks her precious heels. Her feet draw closer, the sandal with the yellow base and the red band hooking her toe, the sandal now sliding off and flicking sand from the ground to the back of her precious legs.

She really does not care for much but her own motion, her own breath, her weightless courage to be loved. Thenjiwe forgives the desire sparkling in her own fine limbs as she hears each whistle penetrate the air and move in her direction. She catches and holds it. She sees a single spotted plume dive down from the marula tree and land in her path. She feels naked and wonders if he, too, has noticed that glittering plume. She wants to pick it up but does not. That would be a risk. She has no confidence that she could bend her knees that far down, stretch her arm, and still be able to come up for air. She would perish, for sure, with him watching, with him able to blow her ashes off the ground with a single breath.

He is totally new to her thoughts, this man; he makes her dizzy. He makes her reconsider each action as though he has a power to form an opinion of her. And why does it matter? She has always just lived her life, with a bit of set pattern. He is different.

Winter, June and July, is her own abode, her own accolade, a pristine time guarded jealously. October. Then rain time, from November to January. The rainy season of mud and insects caught in melting anthills, numerous and silver-winged, transparent-feathered, sliding boulders and crumbling clouds, burrowing earthworms and black beetles with gray-streaked coats, red-eyed, raised antennae, seeming dead. Each drop of rain a rendezvous.

That drizzling time of melting anthills; the rain beats the soil till it slides off its mound. Thenjiwe, more beautiful than rain, watches the rain slow the hills, flatten them, leave gaping holes where an anthill, higher than her shoulders and higher than high, used to be; the rain cleaves the air. Ancient mounds, perforated humps of hardened soil that water cannot melt, cling to the side of the sheltering trees, remain imprisoned, the trees high, the bark cracking, the water swelling harmlessly around the firm and fine soil, which clings, dark, to the roof of the mouth, a syrup when you suck on it. *Amavimbandlebe*—a multitude of tiny insects, winged, blind, dashing themselves against each drop of rain, splattering into a white paste on the ground, dizzy and without wings, a multitude of insects rising like glory, ready to die in order to lose their wings, to be buried in rain. The greatest freedom—to shed the possibility of flight. They descend, brown, scattering to the ground. The birds swoop and fall on them; they emerge within each tip of a wing, each arched dive restless, without wings. *Amavimbandlebe*— the multitude that brings a silence to the ears—their journey is silence, their numbers, their sudden release so surprising, so much that they bring blindness not to the eyes but to the ears. They banish hearing, not sight, for sight is a trance. They are unable to resist the journey of flotation and suicide, the descent into darkness. So one sense aids another, suffers for another, deafness for sight. She is thinking rain time, thinking November, as the man follows her, from Thandabantu Store way past the marula tree, so suddenly.

As he stands briefly where the Shoeshine bus has been, he knows that the swing in her walk places a claim on the entire earth. He is part of that earth, so he follows her like a shadow, seeing her enter the narrow footpath to her village, seeing her fail to raise her eyes to meet that fiery horizon breaking all around them.

Thenjiwe moves without hesitation, with lips ripe and forgiving, she, losing gravity from one day into the next, she, finding strength, flung out of each day into the next; she rises, swinging, her mind free. She is surrounded by *amavimbandlebe*, that multitude of wingless insects scurrying beneath her feet, burrowing the ground for a hibernation that will restore their sense of flotation and their desire for distance. To fly in rain once more, first they must be buried. Rain time, from November to January. October. Hot and dust-ridden, saturated with the steadfast intensity of a season almost over. Steady, like the resolve of this man.

She takes the stranger home. She has a lot to forget, so this is all right. She has no idea now, or ever, that some of the harm she has to forget is in the future, not in the past, and that she would not have enough time in the future to forget any of the hurt.

Time is as necessary for remembering as it is for forgetting. Even the smallest embrace of pain needs time larger than a pause; the greatest pause requires an eternity, the greatest hurt a lifetime. A lifetime is longer than eternity: an eternity can exist without human presence.

A man around her knees. That is all she wants, a man touching her knees and telling her his own pursuit, no matter what it is, just some hope of his, however faint. So here he is, this man. And if the man has followed her all the way from

Thandabantu Store like a helpless child, what is she supposed to do? What does a beehive do with a multitude of bees but harbor them and provide each a delicate task, each a shelter? He loves her heels, he says. She lets him follow her home.

He loves her fingernails. He loves each of her bones, from her wrist to her ankle, the blood flowing under her skin. Does she know that tears are flowing under her eyes even if she is not crying, flowing inside her, before her own entry into her own truth? He loves her bones, the harmony of her fingers. He loves most the bone branching along her hip. The sliding silence of each motion, tendons expanding. The stretch of time as she moves one foot after the next, slowly, and with abandon. White bone her inner being, her hip in motion. He places his palm along her waist and announces, as though she is a new creation, "This is a beautiful bone."

Does she know that bone is the driest substance of being, like all substantial forms that give form, that support wet things such as flesh and water and blood? Bone: the only material in us that cracks, that fractures, that can hurt our entire being, that breaks while we are still living. This he loves, this bone in her, as it is the deepest part of her, the most prevailing of her being, beyond death, a fossil before dying.

He takes her whole wide foot and folds it into his palm. He presses hard on the bone, pushing outward on her ankle till she feels an ache grow and move straight up her hip, where he has been, to every place he has been, where he wishes to be. He takes her fingers in both his hands and folds them into a ball. Her bones fold as she expects them to. The bones beneath her breasts, a cage for memory.

Thenjiwe lets him follow her on that road from Thandabantu Store, leads him across that hot tar and the intoxicating smell of marula seeds falling everywhere. It is a season of marula. The ground is bright yellow with their peels. The ground is hard with their seeds. He picks his way, as she has done, beyond any sweetness the marula could afford if he were to linger and try their soft liquid.

He has been sitting at Thandabantu Store, watching her, and when she notices and does not look away but looks right back, he understands that she has offered him her hips, her laughter, her waiting thighs. What he does next is spectacular and welcome: he follows her home like a shadow.

She does not catch the sound of any of his footsteps because of the blood pumping all the way through her body, bone sliding on bone, her limbs moving. In any case, he places his foot where she has left her imprint on the soil, wanting to possess, already, each part of her, her weight on soft soil, her shape. He wants to preserve her in his own body, gathering her presence from the soil like a perfume.

He loves her breasts, her thirty-two-year-old slope, firm, just as when she was fourteen or whenever it was she first woke to the scent of her own flesh, knowing at once that she was not a man.

She takes home the man who gives her all her hips, who embraces her foot, who collects her shadow and places it right back in her body as though it were a missing part of herself, and she lets him gaze into her eyes till they both see stars through their tears. Gazing into the deep dark pool of her eyes, the man sees places he has never been, she has never been. She drops her arms and lets him encircle her with his arms, with his cool breath, his calm being, till her back succumbs and she folds her arms to her chest and lets each of her elbows seek him out, behind her, where he stands circling her. He frees the entire weight of her body except for her elbows, which he keeps and claims. He warms these with his beating heart, guiding her down to the floor, her mind heir to an eternity. She takes this lover home and gives him a few labors.

He counts each circle of bone on her back. She knows that her emotion is perfect; it is backbone-true. She wishes to conceive a child from this man. He would be a dream child from head to toe. She would name him Mazhanje.

Mazhanje is the name of a fruit from Chimanimani, in the eastern highlands, whose seed this man has brought stuck to the bottom of his pocket, then planted it in her mouth like a gift, days and days after they have met. She has stopped considering time and only considers him.

With the tip of her tongue, she slides the seed around, intending to spit it out into some corner of the room, some dark space where it can lie unclaimed till, with a desire to tidy her mind and her shelter, she sweeps it away with a broom; dried, tasteless, the vanishing evidence of a single encounter with a singular man. However, with one touch of her tongue tip, she loses the rest of her senses. After she has sucked the dryness off it, she is breathless. Breathless.

Mazhanje. Thenjiwe flicks the seed to the roof of her mouth and pushes the man aside, way off the bed. She has been hit by an illumination so profound, so total, she has to breathe deeply and think about it some more. She wants to lie down, in silence. She wants a pause as cool as a valley. The seed in her mouth is sudden and sweet. She wants to sink into its sweetness. She breathes deeply. Solitude.

She forgets his name.

She never wants to be reminded of the name again till he tires of her and wakes one morning and catches that Kezi-Bulawayo-Kezi bus without even looking back at her waving arms, which are asking him to stay. He has tired of a woman who no longer has an interest in his full name, but gives him instructions with her body, turning her full weight over to his side of the bed in order that they touch each other, sliding her palm against his for a greeting, turning his fingers over and bringing them to her quiet tongue; the tip of her tongue licking the moisture off the bottom of his neck, raising her knee high to his navel in order to seek his comfort, gazing kindly at him to draw his body nearer, each embrace offered mutely; parting her legs, offering him the silent but astounding warmth of her thighs.

She never calls him by his name again; this truth he observes, absorbs, and then flees from her magnanimous silence. He leaves before she has said he can, before the rain has stopped beating all around her. He leaves with all that rain around her and no man to hold her while the lightning leaves the sky, and the anthills, melting.

He has to leave even if he is fascinated with her and has not yet figured out all she is about, not even her silence. He remembers how on that fateful day when he followed her from Thandabantu Store to her home, she never looked over her shoulder, but he knew that she knew he was walking behind her all the time. He knew, the way she held her head high. The way she swung to a stop at the end of the pathway and laughed out loud. Her head in the sky. Talking to him without even turning her head. She knew about him and his need. She must have recognized him the way he had recognized her, except he had attached his future to hers, instantly, and she had not. He marveled, the way he saw her in his mind, moving past him while he held a rainbow high up in the sky and she passed beneath it. How he wanted to provide her nothing less than a multicolored sky. Of course she wanted him to follow her all the way along that well-worn footpath with its low grass brushing both their heels; wherever he placed his placid heels, hers had already been.

As he contemplated her presence from the height of that tin can, he knew if she was living in a place called Kezi, and if this was the place called Kezi, and if this place had an imprint of her, a touch of her zeal, then Kezi was a place he could love and get used to. So he followed her all the way home, though he had just disembarked from the bus and was just waiting to get on it again back to the city, and well, Kezi was a place he had been told about, where the bus could carry you to and if you befriended the bus conductor, you could return at half price and tuck a full twenty-pack box of Kingsgate cigarettes in your top left pocket, and keep one cigarette on your lower lip, unlit, all the way back to the city, and if you chose, light it, tap the ash out the window after the schoolchildren and egg sellers had gone by. He wanted to see Kezi, to see more than Bulawayo, after coming all the way from Chimanimani; he wanted to see the mopani shrubs, the Mtshwankela, the Dololenkonyane, the balancing Matopo hills, the gigantic anthills of Kezi. Thenjiwe had made him stay, he was certain, even though she had not said anything precise, nothing in words, but the way she, without parting her lips, held his attention. She was beautiful. True. It was not the details of her face, not the elegance of her neck, the shape of her lips, the nose, the height and force of her limbs, the earth brown skin, not that; more than that. He let the bus leave for Bulawayo without him, even though he had befriended the conductor and already had his half-price ticket in the left pocket of his checkered shirt.

Barely two months, and now all she wants to know is the name of the fruit caught between her teeth. Just that and nothing more. Nothing about him. Only the lost flavor of that fruit. She is possessed by the dry sweetness she has roused from its hard skin. Her tongue seeks it like comfort. And now she makes love to him, with panic and envy, as though he is an unreliable lover. She rises out of his embrace only to sip some water held in a tin cup on the side of the bed and to ask him on what soil the mazhanje grows, how long before each new plant bears fruit, how fertile its branches, how broad its leaf. She rises to ask what kind of tree the seed comes from, the shape of its leaves, the size of its trunk, the shape of its branches, the color of its bloom, the measure of its veins. Does it indeed bloom? Which animal feeds on its fruit, on its leaves, and can its branches bear the weight of a child, more than that, more than a child? Could it grow on the edge of a cliff, on a hanging incline? Near a river? Inside a river?

First, he answers each question patiently, knowing he will be rewarded by a sudden flash of gratitude in her eyes as the mazhanje tree is brought into being. Then he is impatient with this passion and this desire, which takes her more and more away from him, from their touch and caress, from their moments of peace. Which takes her away. Certainly. It is in her eyes, which no longer look at him. Past him. Looking into his pocket for bits of leaf, of sand, the skin that has fallen off this fruit. She lives, now, under its skin. Wanting nothing else but more, and more, of the mazhanje tree. Had he plucked this fruit himself, with his fingers, which she was holding in her own? Had he? He fails to remember that or anything else, so she puts his fingers away, gently.

One day, she draws a resemblance on the ground and asks for the shape of its roots. She wants to know the shape of the roots of this tree. He says he knows nothing about that. He has no business looking at the roots of trees: tentacles. He pushes her away, and her voice, asking about the roots. She asks for each detail as though pleading for mercy.

Instead of holding on to him and letting their love be what it can be, she slides off the bed and stands away from him; her large arms hold to her waist, not letting anything be what it can be, not even their touch. She asks him again about the roots. Thenjiwe knows that the roots of trees have shapes more definite than leaves.

She prods him; she tries to make him remember. She makes him promise to dig up one of these trees when he returns to his village and send her a letter, by bus, on the Kezi-Bulawayo-Kezi route. If it is addressed to Thandabantu Store, it will reach her quickly. The owner, Mahlathini, will send a child with the letter the minute the conductor of the Shoeshine Bus Service hands it to him. Of course, she is already sending him away.

She takes a piece of paper half burned from the fire and blows the flame out. Then she spreads it carefully on the floor, near the firelight. She holds the paper down with her elbow. Using a piece of charcoal, she makes a pattern for him of all the roots she knows. Some of the roots are thick, smooth, lost treasures between a man and a woman. These rise toward the trunk like palms held up, like veins on the earth, capillaries. Some roots spread farther and farther apart, and it is clear that though they have the same source, they will never touch again. These are the strongest roots of all. She slips the paper with her drawings under her body and rises to meet him as he holds her and loves her. She has tears in her eyes. He pulls her away from the fire onto the mat and holds her firmly under his body till the fire is vanished and the light from the fire is vanished and they are alone in the room. The room is dark. The room quiet, the shape of their bodies also vanished. Like the fire. Her voice, naked in the dark, unable to locate form or shape, of tree or man, is vanished, too. The fire is in their bodies, merged, by the dark and silence.

Before he leaves her, he washes her body with milk. He brings the milk in a horn and pours that all over her body. Then he scoops the milk off with both his hands while her arms are held up past her shoulders; the milk trickles white against her dark skin. As he watches her body soak in that liquid, he speaks.

"You are beautiful like creation. Nothing exists that is more beautiful than you. Nothing I can hold. No one is like you. When I strip wet bark off a tree and it slides off distinct and separate like skin, the soft space between the bark and the stem is so pure, I could lick it. No single fleck of dust has ever been near, and it has never breathed the sun, never breathed day; no one has ever laid eyes on it but me. I feel like that when I look in your eyes. Nothing has ever been but your eyes. Nothing."

His every word to her is true. He offers it like a gift. It is his way, this milk, of turning her into that soft bark.

"I want to wash your body with drops of dew. If I could gather all the dew from all the grass along that path we walked on from Thandabantu Store, I would, and pour that liquid over your back. We must meet and love in the grass, one early morning before anyone is about, with the rocks of Gulati watching us from above. It would be as though I had poured the dew over your body, drop by drop. Then we will bask in the first rays of the morning sun. And the dew will ease from our backs. We will lie still and listen to the rays splash out from the sky.

We will watch as the sun dries each single blade of grass and every insect wing, translucent. When we hear the locust flutter its wings, our dance in the dew will be over."

He cups her toes with his hand, these toes, which have already felt the dew. She moves her toes toward him, and this makes him stay his hand over them, longer.

"When I am not touching you, I am nothing. I am not whole. I see nothing. I hear nothing. I am a leaf tossing in the wind. Nothing is as beautiful as your skin."

He is leaving her, but she does not hear it in his voice. She does not hear at all his leaving, desperate voice, even though he goes on and says, "If you died and I could only save one part of your body, I would save this bone. I would carry it with me everywhere, and it would be as though you were alive. Death is when every part of us vanishes, especially the most precious part. We are here. You are in this bone, and it is my most precious memory. When you move, its motion tells me something intimate about your mind. I am inside you. If you die in my absence and I find that you have already been buried, I will dig your body up to the moonlight, so that I can touch this beautiful bone. Touch it, touch it, touch it, till you are alive. Then I will let you rest. With my fingers on your bone. I tremble to imagine you not here, somewhere in the world, when I am alive, somewhere in the world. What do you think? Thenjiwe."

He places his hand on the arc of bone and lets it rest there. He calls her. She does not answer. She has said nothing throughout. He realizes that she is listening to that lonely sweetness she has already found, not him. She has not heard him. She is one of those women who never miss dawn; it resides in their arms. Her silence sifts into the room like fine dust. He slides from light to shadow. He has to. He decides to leave this body of milk and dew and mazhanje seeds. Leave it as apart as it already appears to be, as fulfilled, without his voice disturbing its silence. He leaves with a terrible thirst in his own bones, of loving her.

She loves him but wants to rid herself of a persisting vision of him, a passerby, a stranger sitting at Thandabantu Store, swinging, swinging his knees and whistling a wicked and irresistible tune, casting his glance this way and that, and holding the earth still. She wants emotion of another kind; more than that, she wants to be alone with him, find him again in their silences, and know him with an intense knowing that she herself would never wish to escape. She wants to nestle into him, to forget everything, including Thandabantu Store, whenever she closes her eyes and tries to recall his eyes, his hips, his voice alluring. She would start, perhaps, with the marula tree. She wants to discover the shape of its roots and show them to him till these roots are no longer under the ground but become the lines planted on his palms, each stroke a path for their dreaming. She knows that if she finds the shape of these roots, at least, he would know a deep truth about her land, about Kezi, about the water buried underneath their feet. He would never forget the marula, the scent of its roots and the watery smoothness of a tongue full of seed sliding over and under the senses as you suck it sweet and dry. The flavor of that would never leave his lips or desert the cave of his mouth.

Till he could relish that taste and know the shape of these roots, how can he, with truth and abandon, ever proclaim to linger, to love her as absolutely as she desires to be loved, as knowingly, with all his mind intact, not wandering off to his own tree, to his own slope and incline, to his mountains in the eastern highlands, where that mazhanje grows and beckons him to return? How can he promise to linger without having seen the thornbush suffused with bloom, not knowing about giraffes feeding on leaves the size of a whisper till satisfied and able to hold their heads up above the bluest sky? Him, not knowing the wonder of that, how could he be so sure he could stay as long as that, not having seen nor harvested caterpillars feeding on mopani leaves, not having witnessed their mutable flights, their wondrous turn, and tasted their succulence by her fireside? Him, not having seen the leaves of the mopani emerge and redden the tree, shape into wings not green but a tender maroon, and seen their roots running through the sandiest soil in Kezi, the driest, the most porous soil, with a color like buried bone.

Thenjiwe wants him to stay till he has met her sister, Nonceba, who is away at boarding school, finishing her last year, and who will be here in the first week of December to stay, and be able to meet him; for him to see Nonceba gather the most beautiful flowers from the river and spread them all over the house as she always does, only then can he, too, hear an antelope leap across full streams, as Thenjiwe does at the thought of her only sister, Nonceba, always. In the aftermath, rain. Her mind is traveling back, before this moment, wanting him to travel with her and watch her play with Nonceba in the streams those many years ago, when they are both little and their bodies quiver with delight as they fall into the surface of the river, making the water sing; the Kwakhe River swallows their bodies like boulders, the water circles them, and the heavy raindrops push open their eyelids. The water is warm to the skin, but the river is a rumble, sudden, and they hold hands and rise out of the current to the bank; their laughter is so high, it reaches the hills of Gulati. They watch hornbills swoop beneath tree branches and rise, firmly, into the rocks of Gulati. Only then.

Thenjiwe wants him to hear their two voices together, so that he will know, as tenderly as she does, that before he occupied all the places in her mind, Nonceba, her sister, had already been holding her hand quietly and forever. She runs through cultivated fields; the earth new, with the scent of honey wafting in the air, and the clouds, the rain overhead, and Nonceba.

Nonceba. She who is patient like a mantis, who has no sudden impulses, slow and careful in everything, as though she moves on a delicate ray of light—yes, a mantis in sunlight. That is why she, Thenjiwe, always has to take her sister's hand and run straight into the fields, and not let go, not till Nonceba is running ahead of her, free of her fingers, with all the colors of the sun in her heart. Nonceba, who, though different, is also she, Thenjiwe. Then he would know all of her being, her sister nearer to her than her own shadow, who is her own breath flowing into her body. He needed to stay first, a little longer, then tell her again about his desire to wake, to die, to be reborn in her graceful arms.

This is not what he hears her say. He misses both their particular claims. He breathes slowly and low and separates himself from her. He does not hear her silent song and leaves in order to protect her own truthful search, which he dares not understand nor disturb, certainly not to defend himself or to escape from her, but to respect what he has interrupted. He remembers breath by breath the movement of her, feeling her in the darkness and seeing her as though the room were full of

THE STONE VIRGINS 🪶 49

light, knowing her beauty, in darkness or light. Her neck is
graceful in the darkness, moving slowly toward him, under
his palm spread and held over her, turning her to him, to his
own lips and movements. Nearness: to feel, to see. To touch,
her pulse under his palm, and both their lives in her. This he
sees. This he desires. This he holds dear as they turn, in each
other's arms. She is restless in or out of his arms. In leaving
her, he feels the earth open and swallow him whole. He takes
the first turn out of the room and recalls each of her foot-
prints on that same ground on which he once followed her,
his foot encased in her footprint, and he is already loving her
as he always would, or would want to, or would never be able
to teach himself not to. He leaves her and loves her still. She
hands him back that single seed he brought from his own
land, and it is glistening like a jewel because she has kept it in
her mouth for so long, a seed ready to be planted elsewhere,
not here, since she knows nothing about its roots, and if it can
survive the most permeable soil in Kezi, the driest, and her
tongue craving its memories.

The best love is brief and intense.

The women want to take the day into their own arms and embrace it, but how? To embrace the land and earth, the horizon, and triumph? To forget the hesitant moment, death, the years of deafness and struggle? The women want to take the time of resignation, of throbbing fears, and declare this to a vanished day, but how? And take the memory of departed sons, and bury it. But how? To end the unsure sunsets, the solitary loveliness of the hills? Instead, nothing moves. The rocks remain solid as ever; the boulders are still. Not different. The trees are bare of leaves and carry a stunned and lethargic silence. The women expect sudden and spectacular fissures on the rocks. They expect some crack, some sound that will wrap over them like lightning and they will not need to ask if independence is truly here, or if indeed this is a new day. The women feel an immense pride. They burn in it. This is the most exalting feeling they have for those who have returned, the most protective; they have endured the most agonizing absence, and this feeling is the most understanding emotion, the most accepting, the least demanding, the clearest, the least desperate, the most merciful, born of terror, this pride, filled with glory and tenderness.

A burden lifts as a new day appears. This new day. A place to start again, to plant hope and banish despair, to be restored. Everything is changed. Day is light, not heavy; light as a leaf. The women move from every weaving and meandering pathway, in and out, onto the main road so that the day can find them, find their bodies, which are longing to be touched by something new. They remove bright scarves from their heads and toss them like butterfly wings. They greet the air in red, blue, and green cloth intertwined. The cloth twists under the arms raised, and fingers searching. Their hair is young, even if it has turned white with waiting. For years, they have only learned to wave their voices, from door to mirror, with no hope of release, and now they can dance in the clouds. They wave their arms like promises. They swing their scarves from arm to arm. Shout, and watch their own voices ripple high into the sky, to the hills of Gulati.

They sing earth songs that leave the morning pulsating. They weep in daylight, surrounded by ultrablue skies and the smell of rain. Their minds a sweet immersion of joy, they float, jubilant. Their senses almost divine, uplifted; their pain inarticulate. Voices rise to the surface, beyond the dust shadows that break and glow, and lengthen. They will not drown from a dance in the soaring dust, from the memories of anger and pain. They will not die from the accumulation of bitter histories, the dreams of misfortune, the evenings of wonder and dismay, which should have already killed them. The echoes from Gulati, which should have already killed them. The despondency, to tremble when a door is tightly shut, when it opens wide. A door, a mind. The dust turning into vapor above the distant rocks, which should have destroyed their minds but did not. Today, they walk on a dry earth, not dead, in an intoxicating brightness, and leave no trace of fears, embraced by the day overflowing, touching branches and the tops of trees, a day veined, alive, not dead, replete with wonders and new destinies. They rejoice in a vast sweetness and sound. All that is bright among them is brighter still: the sky, the altars in Gulati, hope. A wind sweeps through the hills, their voices, their bodies in chorus. Their voices wake the somnolent dove. It flies through the dancing light above. Independence will not come again, and the best spectacle of it is in these women, with the pain in their backs, the curve of their voices, and their naked elbows beating the air.

The young women abandon their age mates who are afraid to be with them in quiet places, and who insist on meeting at the bus station and in the presence of their protective mothers. These young women approach Thandabantu Store with a new and purposeful gaiety. They do all they can to discover what their own harrowing impatience is about, and can it be halted, somehow? Can it be stilled and satisfied? Freely and willingly, they slide beside men as old as their oldest brothers, who have returned from the war with all their senses intact, except for that faraway, traveled look that makes the girls a bit fearful, a bit dizzy, a bit excited, that makes them feel brave, as though they are sliding their hands in the cotton-soft coolness of ash, where, it is possible, a flame might sparkle and burn. These solid men suddenly in their midst make their mothers mist, tearful with the wonder of their safe return. They are here. They wear lonely and lost looks but have a touch wild as honey. Their arms and hair are washed with leaves of mint. They refuse neat portions of Lifebuoy and Lux soap bought especially for them from Thandabantu Store and wash their bodies with herbs from the hills, from the river, like modest beings. They guard their loneliness. Their shoulders glow with the last rays of the sun. The women worship these men who lead them all the way to that final place they want to be and which has long been in their minds.

These women, lively and impatient, have secured a freedom that makes their voices glow. They know everything there is to know about anything there is to know, and have tasted their own freedom mature, because it is truly theirs, this freedom. They have not misunderstood. They hold that freedom in their arms. With imaginations unencumbered, they will have children called Happiness, called Prosperity, called Fortune, called True Love, called More Blessing, called Joy, called Cease-fire. Why not? The names will cascade like histories from their tongues . . . Beauty, Courage, and Freedom. All their children will be conceived out of this moment of emancipation. Born into their arms like revelations, like flowers opening. It will be necessary to give their offspring middle names that will provide them strength . . . Masotsha, Mandla, and Nqabutho. Names to anchor dreams.

These women are the freest women on earth, with no pretense, just joy coursing through their veins. They have no desire to be owned, hedged in, claimed, but to be appreciated, to be loved till an entire sun sets, to be adored like doves. They want only to be held like something too true to be believed. They want to know an absolute joy with men who carry that lost look in their eyes; the men who walk awkward like, lost like, as though the earth is shaking under their feet, not at all like what the women imagine heroes to be; these men who have a hard time looking straight at a woman for a whole two minutes without closing their own eyes or looking away; who smile harmless smiles, which make the women weak at the knees and cause them to fold their arms over their heads.

This man seems to say he has not killed anyone, that this is just talk because the country needs heroes, and flags, and festivities, and the notion of sacrifice. Does she not know that? His tone is pleading for her to stop examining his wounds and hindering his view of the hills. At the start of each new day, the question is on her lips, unspoken. Did he? Did he kill a white man?

He gives her a can of sardines and then a yellow ribbon to weave through her plaited hair, and asks her if she is going to be a schoolteacher and teach their children to say *a e i o u* with their mouths shut. He does not stop there with his questions. He asks if it is fine if he contributes to the making of these children, now, under this tree with its arm touching the ground, beneath this warm rock that has absorbed a whole day, under this syringa bush with its petals fanning the air, here, under this open sky, upon the sands of the Kwakhe River, the driest soil there is throughout Kezi and beyond, and surely this river sand sucking their feet in can keep any kind of secret, including their own. And the woman surrenders all the freedom in her arms, nods her head within that softness of night, and accepts those thighs that have climbed slippery rock and the most severe hills of Gulati. Peace and calm pervade every nook, every crag, and surge through her waiting heels.

It is only when he sleeps, his arms flailing about, his voice darker than night and lit with stars, that the woman awakes and pins him down. Then she knows that her journey with this man is long and troubled, and that she cannot keep leaving him each night to his dreams. She is frightened, excited, lost. This man sleeps, but his eyes are open wide. In the morning, she is not looking at him, but at the circling hills of Gulati. She could never suggest it. Even if he smiled and told her the truth about everything, she could never suggest it—that he take her out there to see the hills up close, to touch distant rock, distant water and sky, to drop into the vast space where his mind has wandered through, falling, constantly, even as she moves her lips and whispers his name on her tongue. She could never suggest it, of course not. Not even without saying it, without thinking it. Not even if he said it himself. Lying next to him under the shadow of night is as far from Kezi as he is going to take her. As near to smooth rock and to the torrent of stars out there. She cools his feet, unlaces, pulls, twists the worn and weathered leather boots off him.

The women who return from the bush arrive with a superior claim of their own. They define the world differently. They are fighters, simply, who pulled down every barrier and entered the bush, yes, like men. But then they were women and said so, and spoke so. They made admissions that resembled denials.

They do not apologize for their courage and long absence, nor hide or turn away from the footpath. These women understand much better than any of the young women who have spent their entire lives along the Kwakhe River ever could understand about anything or anyone, and they tell them so, not with words, but they let them know fully and well; they let them speculate, let them wonder what those silent lips are about, what those arms, swinging from hip to shoulder, are about.

These women wear their camouflage long after the cease-fire, walking through Kezi with their heavy bound boots, their clothing a motif of rock and tree, and their long sleeves folded up along the wrist. They wear black berets, sit on the ledge at Thandabantu Store, and throw their arms across their folded knees. They purse their lips and whistle, and toss bottle tops and catch them, and juggle corn husks, which they toss at the young boys, who leap to catch them before they touch the ground. They close their eyes and tuck their berets into the pockets along their legs, button them up, and forget them. From this high plateau, they watch the young women who think freedom can be held in the hand, cupped like water, sipped like destinies. Who think that water can wash clean any wound and banish scars as dry as Kwakhe sand. These women whose only miracle is to watch water being swallowed by the Nyande River after the rain, if it rains, and who mistake the porous sands of Nyande for the substance of their laughter, their reckless joy, their gifts. These young women who possess intact and undisturbed histories, who without setting one foot past the Kwakhe River think they can cure all the loneliness in a man's arms, hold him, till he is as free as the day he was born, till he cannot remember counting the stars overhead, counting each star till he is out of breath and ready to hold his own screaming voice in his hands, to fight. With their immaculate thighs and their tender voices and unblemished skin, they will make a new sun rise and set, so that yesterday is forgotten. Time can begin here, in their arms.

The female soldiers marked with unknowable places on their own faces, with an unquenchable sorrow around their eyes, unaccustomed to a sudden stillness such as this, a sedentary posture and mind-set, no longer wanderers, not threatened or threatening, these women hold their peace and say nothing to condemn or negate, but keep their distance awhile to gather all the evidence they can about the others' cherished hope. This is a cease-fire. When they can, they will avail themselves of destinations. The only sign they give of disapproval is to shake their heads sideways and look long and well as the young women walk into Thandabantu Store in their petticoats or with broken umbrellas to purchase some cream, some Vaseline, wearing leather sandals or with bare feet. They wait before they say anything or pass an opinion. They chew bubble gum, bought by the handful from Thandabantu.

They stay in their camouflage and pull out cigarettes and smoke while standing under the marula tree. They hold their faces up and seem amused either by the sky or by passersby—their mothers. They walk leisurely to Thandabantu Store, slowly, as though they have a lifetime to consider what independence is all about, a lifetime to place one foot after another, a lifetime to send a ring of laughter past the wing of a bird. They have no haste or hurry, no urgent, harrowing hunger to satisfy, no torment they would rather not forget. Independence is a respite from war; the mind may just rearrange itself to a comfortable resolution, without haste, at the pace of each day unfolding and ending naturally, and opening again like a flower.

They sit on empty crates, like the men, then from here they watch the sun as though the watching of a sunset is simply a soothing pastime; but watching the sunset from Thandabantu Store and watching the sunset from the bush with a gun in your hand are related but vastly different acts. They are learning, with patience and goodwill, how it is to watch the sunset from Thandabantu. To watch a sun setting without a gun in your hand, so in this fair pursuit they forget that they are male or female but know that they are wounded beings, with searching eyes, and an acute desire for simple diversions. It is an intimate quest.

The men who for years have been going to Thandabantu to watch the sun, to summarize the day and what they have just heard of the war in the bush, who are part of the quality of this veranda and the sound of it and therefore an essential aspect of a place named Kezi because Kezi starts and ends at Thandabantu Store, these Kezi men have moved without reluctance or amazement at their displacement, moved to the marula tree and brought their hand-carved stools with them, and from here they watch these women exude an elegance more spectacular than anything they have ever watched set or burn, their posture more genuine than their own feet on Kezi soil. They watch from the corners of their eyes, feeling tongue-tied and charmed and privileged. And these men, whose feet have never left the Kwakhe River or wandered anywhere farther than Thandabantu Store, lower their eyes frequently and efficiently, and their shoulders, too, and pull their torn and faded hats farther down. Thus contrite, they glance at those military shoes, at those arms like batons, and look straight away, enchanted but not betrayed. They avoid those eyes or those hips under those clinging belts. The breasts, held carelessly up, as though they are nothing but another part of the body where some human life just might be nurtured and survive, the breasts only a shape on the body, like the curve of the shoulder, a useful but wholly unremarkable part of the anatomy. The men know but dare not discuss how those breasts have held guns, have held dreams, and that they could never hold anything overnight less burdensome, less weighty than a broken continent.

The Kezi bus arrives in the late afternoon, as usual. It is dust-ridden, creaking, and sinking its weight of people and possessions downward and then way up the bridge to the sudden end of the tarred road; the wheels hit the dirt road and dig and slide out of it, sideways toward the marula tree; the cloud of dust is thick with the sound of abrupt wheels. The sudden stop. The weight. These women view the men getting off this Shoeshine bus and neither smile nor curse. Their look is complacent; their thought is undisturbed. The men who have arrived from Bulawayo walk with bold and curious steps into the store. They pause on the first step, caught by nonchalant voices. They go in. They emerge with open bottles of Fanta and cream soda.

They lean on pillars and cautiously look around and examine the air. They have read enough and know that these women are not mere pictures from the newspapers folded under their arms, papers announcing a landslide victory for the new prime minister, but beings they could greet with care and due respect. But they do not. These women have known the forest in rain and sun, survived its darkness and light, equally threatening. These women, alive now sitting on the edge of this smooth wall, are the most substantial evidence of survival there is, of courage, of struggle. Alive now and looking right past their own shoulders, as though they are invisible beings, interested in the things beyond, the secret things that only their minds have known, alive here now and as close to their bodies as their own perplexed and curious minds can endure. Survivors, sitting here now, on this veranda, today, looking terrific and undisturbed, as though they have just been away somewhere fine, picking wildflowers from some gentle groove of the earth. No, their fingers are not made for delicate acts like that; they have just been away overnight somewhere. Somewhere dark enough that when they return, as they have, they carry this dark place in their gaze. They are so impenetrable, the Bulawayo men can only wait for them to say something first, but they meet a dead silence.

If they could speak first and exchange a few words with them, it would be like touching the same leaves in the forest that these women have touched, the same branches; the skies they have seen would also be here on this veranda. The men keep their distance, lean even farther away from these women, from their penetrating gazes, unsure of words, the tone of voice necessary to be tolerated, to be indulged, to gain the response of these mighty and serene women whom nothing seems to disturb. The killing of doves, is it different in the forest? They would like an account of something simple like that, an answer about killing doves. If they placed their question carefully like that, innocently, plainly, perhaps they would get an answer that would satisfy all their questions. Did they kill doves, and if so, how? If they started by asking about the doves, could it not be that some other revelation would tumble out, a truth they could not even imagine, some astounding fact that would gain them their own legitimacy, some facet about this war beyond their own conception? Instead of asking this one question, they are gathering the shape of these women into a treasurable memory, knowing they owe them too much even to begin to speculate; to owe a woman a destiny is more than their minds can deal with right now, under this veranda. To owe desire, that would be quick and easy, but life, its pattern and progress, this they quickly banish and return their minds to examining the burnished, glossy, dark skin of these undisturbed women whose charity is equal to their capacity for harm. Their fascination is irresistible, and the men watch, and sip their drinks, and move into Thandabantu Store to deliver empty bottles, and return to slide down with their wares and sit on the cement floor, since all the crates are occupied. The fingers peeling skin off sweet marula fruit, how many lives have vanished into those arms, how many doves?

The men stare and let themselves be enamored by the possibilities of freedom. Who would have thought that one day, within this confined place, they would congregate with women fighters and listen to the soccer score between Highlanders and Dynamos announced over portable radios while they stand stunned to silence, unable to imagine anything at all they hold in common, not even independence or the soccer score, nothing to discuss. They panic, knowing there will never be a time like this again and that the next time they see these women they will no longer be these women and no moment at all like this will continue to exist and that this is the only time that can make the air tremble and their own voices vanish and when no words can be found to greet a woman at noon. No words at all. They fumble and fail. With disbelief at their own inability, they submit to a lengthening silence. They linger, too curious to walk away, yet too afraid to speak, too inferior in some intimate detail of existence, some risk they have not taken. They stand like apparitions. They want to ask if any of them ever met any of the new leaders of the country and shook hands with them. They dare not ask some personal and frenzied detail like that and so bury the question in their mouths. They lean on those pillars and stand their ground, claiming some part of this veranda. They linger, like moths to flame.

A breeze stirs the air. The women love this shade as cool as water could be.

1981—1986

Streetlights and luminous balconies, doorways, drinking houses, tailor shops, bus stops and fish-seller porches. Shoemakers in makeshift shelters. Milkmen in shirts with torn and faded blue collars, ice-cream vendors chatting to forgetful prostitutes, ambulance drivers, blood drying on their fingernails. Husbands carrying loaves of bread to their lovers, bespectacled priests, dogs barking at half-masked nuns from mission schools. Painted rooftops and bright tower lights. Barbed-wire fences and open-air markets. Naked hips dance Jerusalem dances at the small city hall for the first black mayor. School buses and doorbells. Dragonflies drink from potholes on the Luveve Road. Funeral parlors are scented with hibiscus bushes.

The war begins. A curfew is declared. A state of emergency. No movement is allowed. The cease-fire ceases. It begins in the streets, the burying of memory. The bones rising. Rising. Every road out of Bulawayo is covered with soldiers and police, teeming like ants. Roadblocks. Bombs. Land mines. Hand grenades. Memory is lost. Independence ends. Guns rise. Rising anew. In 1981.

K ezi.

The man places his hand over her left shoulder. Her thoughts turn blind, ashes stirred by a small wind. He presses his hand down on her limp arm. He turns her body toward himself, looking for something in her he can still break, but there is nothing in her that can still be broken. For Nonceba, there is only the scent of this man, the cruel embrace of his arms, the blood brown of his shoes, the length of his neck, and the gaze bending close. The distance in her mind is infinite. No . . . no . . . no . . .

Between them is an absence measured by pauses and suspicious silences. Perhaps, in one of these absences, he may recover and feel something akin to kindness, not pity. It is remote, pity, in a man like this. He may forget why he is here, why she is with him, who she is. He, too, may be stunned by his own dramatic presence.

A knee lifts up to touch the bottom of her legs, from behind her, then slides to her thighs, moving sideways. "Sit here, on my knee." He moves away briefly, carefully, then returns his touch to her body. He returns his touch as though it were something he has taken away without permission, guiltily, yet like a kind act.

He is close, touching her; she knows what he is doing, where his arms are, his legs, his knees, that neck, that voice. Then she is certain of his arms. Only then.

Her thoughts are as precise as his—splinters of glass. It is important to locate his brief absences. She is a caterpillar—she can hide inward, recoil, fold her knees and her elbows, and all the parts of her body that can bend, that are pliable, in her mind.

I am waiting. I am alive, now, a companion to his every thought. I am breathing. My temples, beating. She closes her eyes and her body listens as his movements pursue each of her thoughts. She breathes. Harm.

He enters her body like a vacuum. She can do nothing to save herself. He clutches her from the waist, his entire hand resting boldly over her stomach. He presses down. He pulls her to him. She hesitates. He forces her down. She yields. She is leaning backward into his body. He holds her body like a bent stem. He draws her waist into the curve of his arm. She is molded into the shape of his waiting arm—a tendril on a hard rock.

He is at the pit of her being. Her anger rises furiously. Her saliva is a sour ferment of bile. She would like to speak, to spit. She swings forward, away from him. He is close. A knee, a shoulder, a leg, moving over her own thighs. His arm is moist, warm, the scent rising from each of his motions is a thick paste of desire.

He pulls her body up and holds her still. As suddenly, her thighs feel pain, a hot liquid coursing down to her own knees.

He draws her entire body into his own. Mute. He is a predator, with all the fine instincts of annihilation. She, the dead, with all the instincts of the vanquished.

To survive ambush. These are her thoughts, hot fluid floating. She follows the force of his hand like a map and walks backward, heel-first, the journey longer and longer as she listens to the surprising pain. Her legs moving. Step . . . back . . . step . . . back . . . only her toes reach the ground. He drags her. She moves on her toes, backward, with no weight on them, with all her weight in his arms, with the force of his presence swirling in her mind. Her heel is above his shoe, weighing down, her arm in his arm.

She holds on. Has she lived before this moment of urgency and despair? Is there something whispered before a cataclysmic earthquake, sleep, before a frightful awakening to death? Is life not lived backward, in flashes, in spasms of hopeless regret?

The cruel surface of his body as it accompanies hers, solid. He leads her, moment by moment, to a place that only he has imagined. That cry comes directly from her mind, not from her mouth. Where is he taking her?

He bends. Away from her. He pulls a stool from the entrance of the house, as though getting ready for amiable conversation. Nonceba hears the stool hit the wooden doorway, while the door swings and hits the wall, returns and hits the frame as he again pulls the stool, roughly. The sound of the hinge dims, weakly, near to her. Sound dies like a living thing.

She does not look at him. Her face is turned from him. She is silent, without worth, with nothing precious but time. She is nothing to him. An aftermath to desire.

She feels him inside her body. Near. He is as close as her own tongue, as close as her arms are to her body, her hair on her skin, close like her heartbeat; his breathing is her breathing. She is breathing in. His sweat is in her nostrils. His perspiration.

A jingle in his pocket, coins, keys, what . . .

She falls, sinks into his lap, and meets the hardness of these objects, a bundle jutting, something made of metal, unknown instruments that she fears. He pulls her down into himself, holding on to her wrists, leaning the rest of her body into himself, a companion. His arm is under her left breast, lifting her, pressing into the softness of her being; her nipples are hard, stiff, meeting the rough edges of his fingernails. Her mind is scalded with the presence of his arms.

"Are you afraid to look at me?" he whispers. He cups her chin as though parts of her are crumbling, falling, blowing off with the wind. He turns her and pulls her face close to his own. She is solid. Like a mirror.

His fingers part her lips, dry skin, find her tongue. His fingers are on her tongue . . . move into her mouth . . . over her tongue. He curls his fingers and slides them over the top of her lips.

Her breathing slides between his fingers, her warm saliva. He bends his fingers farther into the warm spaces beneath her tongue. Nonceba tastes him. He is dried salt, a ferment—the dried, dead blood. He scoops her being, her saliva water to cleanse a wound.

She is only a dot in his mind. Something that can vanish.

He places her arms around his neck as though she were a child he would raise in kindness. He rocks back and forth. Forward, rocking back. He seeks the inside of her thighs, her dark skin, hard, over her knees. He holds her dark bone.

"Hold me. Touch me here. Look at me. I said touch me here."

She drops her arms from his neck. His left knee moves back and forth under her thighs. He parts his knees. He parts her knees.

He portions her to a dead past.

Suddenly, he tears the sleeve off her dress and it falls to her elbow, hanging uselessly; white threads dangle from her shoulder.

He waits, patient as an entire season, as disobedience, as a thief. He can see the shape of her disbelief. He owns her like a memory. He is the type to own the intangible— hallucinations, fragrances, death. So, though she breathes deeply, it is with a stillness that he owns, with a hope he has banished. He commands. She dares not contradict him.

He can see past her to that tree bare of leaves. She sits inanimate, a receptacle for his dreaming. She breathes, afraid to shift, to move her back against his arms, afraid to ease her shoulders, afraid. Calm. With desperation.

He cradles her like a wounded child. Nonceba almost believes him, in him, almost removes him and his lullaby from this scene, almost. He offers words that could heal. He closes his eyes and moves his lips against her neck. His words flood her earlobe, slip between her legs, where her blood falls like burnt water. She feels it. He could heal her, shield her with his body. He just could. Her legs hang, empty, within his parted thighs. Then his legs close and hold her tight.

There. With him. His whispers over her neck, heated air. His words move slowly over her. He is so close, she opens her eyes and conquers the darkness burning beneath them. She moves into light. She is floating without direction. She lets her eyelids fall. Darkness descends. Light is sharp. It penetrates.

On the other side of the doorway, where the wall curves and disappears, she sees her sister, Thenjiwe. A part of her. Thenjiwe, fallen, breasts pressed to the ground, bare soles, blind eyes, bent arms folded, legs stretched out, a body pleading, a stillness visible.

I am afraid to close my eyes. I am afraid of myself. I am darkness.

He is an ordinary man, wearing a blue shirt with buttons not white, not black. Gray. Short sleeves. Khaki trousers. A safe attire. A shirt you can trust, with buttons you can trust. Her eyes swallow him whole, the blue patches remaining on his shirt here and there, dry, the rest soaked, pasted against his body like a skin. Here a patch of fabric that matches the sky. Half the collar is folded inward. His skin is taut, glistening. His trousers are frayed at the bottom. Large feet. Shoes. Thick shoelaces. Thick soles.

He means it: he wants to be held by her; he needs it. I will live, she thinks.

"Your fingers are warm. Touch me with these smooth hands. Move your arm this way."

He lifts her legs off the ground and places her across both his knees, like a bride. He guides her thumb to his pulsing temple. An ordinary day. Just the heat. Above, the sound of wings, birds: weightlessness. In the long distance, a dog barks, and dies, and barks. It whimpers, a straggly sound. On such a day, dogs have found new voices. Already the flies are turning the entire ground dark. The blood on the ground. Death.

The creases down his own thick neck are covered with sweat. Now she must put her fingers in his. She is already escaping while his hands are approaching hers. Their fingers touch like a greeting. They touch and hold. He smiles, though not at her, needing to be touched. The sun is hot. The flies are here, turning the sun dark.

I am alive, on this knee. I am waiting. I am alive.

She sees a silver bucket approaching from the bright blue of the sky, carried above the head, her sister's arm holding it up along one side and her fingers curling over the rim of the bucket brimming with water; then the arm drops and the bucket approaches, steady, steady in that teasing blue. Now she can see the bucket leaning over, filled with water, the tiniest drops breaking like a spray, spilling; then the bucket crushes its contents to the ground; water breaks like stone.

The silence that follows is astonishing, quiet, like breathing. She runs forward past the water now vanished, now a patch of dampness and mud. The bucket is in the sky. Nonceba's mind is loose like a whip. She retreats, moves back from the water splashing forward toward her naked feet, vanishing into her mind.

"Thenjiwe . . . " she calls. A man emerges. He is swift. Like an eagle gliding.

His head is behind Thenjiwe, where Thenjiwe was before, floating in her body; he is in her body. He is floating like a flash of lightning. Thenjiwe's body remains upright while this man's head emerges behind hers, inside it, replacing each of her moments, taking her position in the azure of the sky. He is absorbing Thenjiwe's motions into his own body, existing where Thenjiwe was, moving into the spaces she has occupied. Then Thenjiwe vanishes and he is affixed in her place, before Nonceba's eyes, sudden and unmistakable as a storm. The moment is his. Irrevocable. His own.

How did a man slice off a woman's head while a bucket was carried above it? How did a man slice a woman's throat and survive?

Then he holds the dead body up, this stranger, clutching that decapitated death like a rainbow. He holds Thenjiwe up. Then he seems to hold Nonceba's body up, too, for it is impossible for her to continue standing, for her own mind to survive by its own direction. He holds both their bodies up. Frozen.

He slides into the dead body as though into a mute stream. Thenjiwe's blood flows from her body and curls around him, pulsating.

What kind of instrument has he used to cut her head off like that? The head is now dangling on Thenjiwe's breast, separated. The bucket, the water, her own voice running out into the yard, running into the stream of clear water sliding forward from that incredible death. Nonceba keeps her eyes up, in that bluest sky, while her body sinks willingly to the ground, absorbs the fatal agony like water into earth. Her body falls in the same way sound disappears, the way it moves away from one without shifting boulders the way water does, without disturbing even the most weightless object, not the lightest feather, without changing the pattern of stars. Sound departs without substance, like a torn veil lifting, greeting the air, like burning silk.

Her feet are on the ground.

This water is red, mud. My toes are sticking together, sucking the ground. I stand still in this pool of water, with my toes sticking together and the mud red, the red mud, the mud with blood.

What did he use to cut Thenjiwe's head off, so invisibly, so rapidly?

N onceba stands still, suddenly, and her body heaves forward. She has to pull back, pull her feet from the mud red and take a few steps back. The mud red step back.

A few steps and the moment feels immediately like safety, her feet sliding. Memory slips; red, mud, dead.

In that quickness, moments before that, Nonceba sees the right arm pull back and grab the body by the waist, a dancing motion so finely practiced, it is clear it is not new to the performer. It is not the first death he has held in his arms, clutching at it, like a bird escaping. It is not the first death he has caused. The body falls forward and he stumbles and then pulls the body back; bone-bright white flashes, neck bone pure, like a streak of light the bone vanishes into the stream of blood oozing out, the knees buckle forward, and the body twirls on its heels, the legs together, then dragging sideways— a soft ankle held to the ground. He flips the body to his left and the legs turn their weight, and death, over, an ankle held soft and dead to the ground.

He pulls the body back on its heels. The body succumbs. His shoulder is high, determined, his legs together and kneeling forward; he pulls the arms back and holds on to the weight. Everything is still. Nonceba is not breathing. The body is his, pulse and motion. He pulls the arms back, only the arms, and this brings the chest forward, the breasts outward, pushing against that thin cotton cloth of blood. The blood ripples over the breasts.

He stands a long time in this position, unchaining the arms and hoisting the body up just before it collapses, dangling it from his left shoulder. "Thenjiwe . . . " Nonceba calls. "Thenjiwe . . . "

Again he holds. He holds tightly, as though this part of the game requires courage, an ingenious tenderness, this part when his mind dances with a dead body. Then he changes his thought and looks over his shoulder and over the body. He looks all around. Frantic, he turns, heaving the body with him; he turns around again, twice, then stops. His back is turned toward her.

From behind him, she can see the bare arm is limp, as though her sister is simply tired from hard labor. Nonceba longs for the flight of eagles. The flight of thought. There is only discord; release as deaf as stone.

The mud, dead, dried, red. She calls again for Thenjiwe. Dead.

He carries the body spread on his back, an arm limp on each shoulder, his motion forceful, true with blood. He is stepping sideways, and back, forward and sideways. On his back, the body presses down along his spine. He turns steadily, with the movements of a hunter who kills not because he is hungry but because his stomach is full, and therefore he can hunt with grace. He stops. He abandons the body right there where he has been standing, no longer nursing the body, removing this burden from his shoulder instead, throwing it off like a stale thought.

The body is no longer his. The body is hers.

Then he moves swiftly toward Nonceba. He pulls her toward him.

I am alive, waiting on this stranger's knee.

Nonceba moves her left fingers down his arm like a blind woman searching for a man she once met in a dream:

the one who attacked her, who held a flame to her eyes and brought blindness. The flesh swells and ripples down this arm nearest to her. Her fingers continue downward. Here the skin roughens. Dark. Veins swollen. They ripple under the skin. The wrist. The nails are flat, as though they have been held beneath rock for too long. The fingers, burned. This is her only act of courage—to identify his arms.

Then he pulls her down, as though measuring the weight of her thought in his hands. His fingers approach hers. She cannot avoid him. The driest palm is in her palm. The skin on his palm, furrowed. She looks down at her feet, at the red mud. Blood dries quickly, and cracks.

Each measure of touch anticipates a violence she already knows.

His hair, cemetery flowers. That is what Thenjiwe said about hair like this, white and black mingling together, intertwined. The black hair, youth, the white in celebration of death. The head has a way of gathering its own flowers, of gathering time into a bouquet, Thenjiwe says. She, who knew how to gather languages and wisdom with the same mouth. What would she say in such a moment? Who would she be? That was not true about time moving relentlessly forward, leading us toward the grave. Time stands still, like now.

Cemetery flowers never bloom. No one waters them. Wildflowers with strong hearts take any season to bloom. Just to make sure the flower outlives the planter, it must be the sort to bloom fiercely during a drought, shedding petals like old skin. To know this sort of flower, you need to have buried a lover or a child. They were meant to laugh when Thenjiwe said that, to accept the inevitable, the ending of all beginnings, the dying of the wise, who have seen the sun set and rise so many times that the smoke from its flame has turned their hair white. Those who have known such passion and desire that this, too, has burned portions of their memory. Those who have known laughter and made reckless journeys into the mind, into betrayals, and danced with their own shadow at noon. Those who no longer care much for trust, who know absolutely that lust eventually dries up and curls ridiculously like a leaf: it desiccates. Such sentient beings who laugh at death and welcome sleep like an inane gift and then wake as though to the sound of a clanging bell. Those who pluck a sliver of hair like a root, knowing full well the sound of their own feet moving like a slow hallucination to the grave. Those who have seen the bloom fall off trees, who have seen fish mate in rivers and tadpoles lose their tails. They had such hair.

Here was a man with just such hair.

He thinks of scars inflicted before dying, betrayals before a war, after a war, during a war. Sibaso. He considers the woman in his arms.

He sees her dancing heels, her hands chaste dead bone, porously thin, painted on a rock. Her neck is leaning upon a raised arrow, her mind pierced by the sun. She is a woman from very far, from long ago, from the naked caves in the hills of Gulati. She does not belong here. She bears the single solitude of a flame, the shape and form of a painted memory.

He thrusts the body to the ground: a dead past.

Nonceba falls. She spins her head away from him. She falls over her arms, her hands trapped between her breasts. She views him from one side of her body, sees only his shoes. She crawls away, on her stomach, away. Then she is up. He has raised her from the ground.

He holds her face close to his own. His eyes flicker past her like a ray of light. The moment is brief, too lightning-quick, a time before she can question his too-quick action, or act, or move, or think, or wonder what, where is he, what, before all that. Motion by motion, step back, her heel borne on the tip of his shoe, just a fleeting touch is all she feels, not lasting—except the incessant pain afterward. She thinks it is just that, his touch along the chin; instead, it is razor-sharp.

It seemed he had only touched me briefly with the back of his hand, mildly, and moved his right elbow near my left shoulder, raised it high, it seemed then. I did not drop my eye-lids, raise my arm, shout, move away. His motion was simple. It was soft and almost tender, but I did not know that it was no longer his touch tracing my chin, not just a touch on my lower lip, but more than that. For a moment, all this was painless. I felt nothing. He sought my face. He touched it with a final cruelty. He cut smoothly away. He had memorized parts of me. Shape and curve; lips unspoken.

He closes her hand. Her wrist bends, veins striated. Nonceba mourns with a hunger caught between rock and sky. Her mind inert. She shivers, like smoke rising.

Alone, afterward, she turns Thenjiwe's body over and pulls the blouse down to cover the wet breast. Wordless. She slides her fingers under the red cloth. Her touch is warm and longs for life, this lingering heat in the flesh, this threshold. Wordless.

7

His name is Sibaso, a flint to start a flame. Him. Sibaso. I follow him closely. My life depends on it. I follow the shape of his body. I follow his arms. He has killed Thenjiwe. He is in the midst of that death.

I listen, unsure of any of his words, what he means, what he needs, claims, pardons, affirms, but the rise of his voice could mean anything, and silence, an assertion of death.

"Is there anyone here besides yourself? Who else lives here? Do you expect someone? Are you with someone?"

He whispers in my ear, as though someone else will hear his deep secret and uncover his camouflage.

I dare not move. Is he asleep? Is he in an embrace of his past? He knows how to sleep in the midst of any reality, of several realities. He can inflict harm as easily as he can retrieve it. He has lived to tell many illicit versions of the war, to re-create the war. Here he is. Him.

"Spider legs," he insists. In my fear of him, I envy this kind of perfect truth, which sounds exactly like a well-constructed lie. While he closes his eyes, I have the sensation that I am drowning, and see a multitude of spider legs stretch into the darkness. "That is the other strange fact about spiders, their ability to walk on water while humans drown," he says.

Sibaso had eaten handfuls of spider legs throughout the war. He knew where spiders went to die. He knew their alcove of death. "Is this not a great secret to know?" he asks.

There is a tragic innocence that knows nothing but death, that survives on nothing but death.

M y name is Sibaso. I have crossed many rivers with that name no longer on my lips, forgotten. It is an easy task to forget a name. Other names are assumed, temporary like grief; in a war, you discard names like old resemblances, like handkerchiefs torn, leave them behind like tributaries dried. During a war, we are lifeless beings. We are envoys, our lives intervals of despair. A part of you conceals itself, so that not everything is destroyed, only a part; the rest perishes like cloud.

Independence, which took place only three years ago, has proved us a tenuous species, a continent that has succumbed to a violent wind, a country with land but no habitat. We are out of bounds in our own reality.

During a war, it is better to borrow a name, to lend an impulse to history. It is necessary to supply a motive to time, moment by moment, to offer a stimulus. Life has to be lived, even if not believed. A man must grow openly like a tree, with nothing between his cry and the elements. Instead, it is a war, and a man becomes a stalker, always a step behind some uncanny avenue of time, and he follows all its digression, its voyage into tragic places. He finds himself in dark places, unlit sites, dark and grim. A shadow when he walks, a shadow when he sleeps. His mind is perforated like a torn net and each event falls through it like a stone. When he stands, his head hits against something heavy—he discovers that history has its ceiling. He is surprised. He has to crouch, and his body soon assumes a defensive attitude; he possesses the desire to attack. If he loses an enemy, he invents another. This is his purge. He is almost clean. He seems to have a will, an idea that only he can execute. Of course, this idea involves desecration, the violation of kindness. It is a posture both individual and wasteful. He cannot escape. He is the embodiment of time.

There is a type of spider that turns to air, its life a mere gasp. This type of spider gathers all its kin before an earthquake, sending its messages through the air. Together, the spiders gather into a cubicle of time, a bowl in a peeling rock, a basin where the earth has been eaten by rain; this takes place before an earthquake, before the advance of an enemy, and war. Spider after spider piles into a mound, into a self-inflicted ruin, seeking another form of escape. Then the top of the spider mound is sealed with spit, thick and embroidered like lace, bright with sun rays, and rainbows arching like memories. A stillness gathers before an earthquake, before war. There is a stillness such as has not been witnessed before, and a new climate in that trapped air. Turning, again and again, till something is freed, like a kindness. A spider falls like a pendulum stilled. This is not hibernation for a death: the bodies take flight, free as time. The body vanishes, from inside out, the inside pouring like powdered dust, the legs a fossil. This is the end of creation, the beginning of war.

I have harvested handfuls of spider legs while they remained interlocking like promises, weightless, harmless needles. Time's shadow: life's residue. I blow life's remains off my hand like a prediction. On my hand is a dark melody, shapes that curl and twist into thin marks, like tiny words on a page, a hand-written pamphlet, some spilled ink on ancient rock. I wipe my palm clean. Our country needs this kind of hero who has a balm for his own wounds carried between lip and tongue, between thumb and forefinger, between the earth and the soles of his feet, who is in flight toward an immaculate truth.

I have seen a spider dancing with a wasp. This type of spi-der hangs from asbestos ceilings in every township home. Most men watch the motions of such a spider. Every survivor envies a spider dancing with a wasp.

There is a type of spider that changes color when mating. It devours its own partner and rolls him into a fine paste. With this, it courts its next partner. It offers him this round, perfectly prepared sacrifice in exchange for a brief but sweet liaison. This kind of spider hangs between trees and can only be viewed in the light of a full moon. Such a spider possesses a valuable secret—the knowledge that love cannot be founded on mercy but that mercy can be founded on love. It knows the true agony of ecstasy, that violence is part of the play of oppo-sites, and that during war, there are two kinds of lovers, the one located in the past, and dead, the one in the future, living and more desirable. The past a repast, the future a talisman. This kind of truth also belongs to the fantasy of a continent in disarray.

There is a spider with long, long legs that are terrifyingly thin, ready to disappear. This spider is almost transparent, its legs wisps of a dancing dark light, like pencil strokes. The legs keep it high off the ground, and there is nothing to it really, just a pale body. An apparition. I saw it walk across a mirror one morning. Then it stopped moving. The mirror looked cracked. I could see my own broken face behind it. This is a postwar spider, a hungry spider. It is fragile, like the membrane around dreams.

When this spider passes by, it seems as though you could blow its awkward legs with a whisper. The joints upon its legs are mere full stops, abbreviations for a death. Its outline is a parenthesis. You find this spider in the early hours of the morning, gawky, sliding into corners, its body weaving like thread, shining like muslin, like malice. It has no predators. It lives off starvation. Whoever would hunt it would have to lick its invisibility off the ground, like spilled salt. It knows how to live on a margin, brittle, like a shard of glass. Who would want to eat such an already-dead thing? In the future, there will be no trace of it. It dies outside time.

Yes. I am asleep. I feign death, as I did in the bushes of Gulati when a dangerous-looking spider crept over my arm. I would watch it, holding my breath, remaining as still as a rock. There was no mistaking a poisonous spider; all the evidence was there, the legs ferocious, hairy pincers. It had a deadly weight about it, on your arm. A confident weight. It strolled all over your arm like a deranged dancer, outrageous in its design and coloration. You could feel it trying to make a decision, wondering if you were human, and if you were, whether you were already dead. A spider never wastes its venom. You could feel its belly graze your skin. Poised. It made an art out of inflicting harm and approached you in daylight. It had a swiftness about it that seemed not to belong to the species. A lithe body. An elongated design. It lingered suspiciously. If it moved off quickly, then it had granted you a reprieve. The encounter was ironic—death near and far. They have a name for this sort of spider: *umahambemoyeni*—"the swimmer in the air." I thought I had left this sort of spider in the bush, where its charm and dismay belong. Survival is a skill hewn from the harmonies of nature.

He whispers. He mumbles, delirious. He throws me violently to the ground, suddenly. Then he brings me up again, back into his arms. I feel him pressed against my body, only that, then a pain invisible. He throws me back to the ground, and vanishes.

8

A woman screams. Her voice sweeps down the corridor like a hot liquid. Her voice is high. Something pitiful is pouring out of it, something unstoppable. Her voice is muffled, suddenly held down. Many people are holding her down. The woman is destroying a thought in her mind. She is getting rid of something. Only light and sound can cleanse a mind, not touch. She is cleansing her mind. The woman calls endlessly, down and down the corridor. How long is the corridor? How long has the woman been crying? Something is vanishing. Snuffed. She is dying. She is silent. No, her voice is louder. She is alive in the room. Her voice is in Nonceba's mind.

Two people are walking down the corridor. Nonceba does not want to listen to their voices; she is holding on to the broken voice, now distant, of the woman screaming, vanishing, troubled by her own mind dying. But the door is open; she can see past the white sheets of her hospital bed to the light in the passage, and the footsteps are near, slowing down. The burgundy curtain is open, pushed tight to the end of the rail. The window is open only a crack, and outside this large window, a bush of hibiscus is blooming. It is higher than the window, so she cannot see the full height of it. Behind it is a wide concrete ramp. Then an entrance. She listens to the footsteps approaching her doorway. A woman's footsteps. A man's voice. The voices bring strong images to her mind of the woman screaming in the next room, a woman whom she has not seen. Though she is not aware of it, Nonceba has been lying here, in this bed, for a week, with the voice right next to her bed. There.

Nonceba shifts her back. She sinks deeper into the bed. She would like to turn her pillow over. It feels too warm, soiled, damp. Someone has tied her arms down to the metal frame of the bed. She cannot move them. Thick bands bind her body and hold her down. She can move her eyes. She looks outside the room. She looks at the hibiscus blossoms. They have large petals. She does not like red flowers. "Red flowers are the brightest flowers. You must like them." Why is Thenjiwe saying that? Why is she saying that in her head? She, Nonceba, does not like red flowers. They fill up the entire space in the mind. She does not want a flower to do that, to bloom in her head. She likes white-and-yellow flowers. When you place them in your hair or hold them in your arms, they look like flowers, not blood.

The voices in the corridor are nearer now, and the footsteps. They are discussing the woman whose voice they have held down. How long has the woman been dying? How long has she been buried in her own voice? Dying, in her own voice. Held down.

"She has killed her husband. Two soldiers walked into her house and sat her husband on a stone. They handed her an ax. These men were pointing guns at her two grown sons, threatening to shoot them if she did not listen. She fell on her knees and begged them to let her sons go. One soldier pushed her away with the butt of his gun. She fell down and wept for her sons as though they had already died, and for the heart of the soldier, which she said had died with the war. Her husband raised his voice toward her and said, 'Kill me . . . Kill me.' He pleaded. He was desperate to die and to save his two sons. She stood up, silently repeating what her husband had said, with her own lips, with her own arms. She opened her eyes and raised the ax above her shoulders till he was dead. That is what happened to her. The men left her in that state. A dead husband and two living sons."

Now Nonceba can see the woman with the ax. She is tall and thin and her legs do not reach the ground. Her body is suspended in the air. It is as though she is hanging from a tree. "Is she hanging from a tree?" Why does Thenjiwe ask that? Why ask at all? The woman is a tree and all the branches are in her head, moving back and forth. The woman wants to cut the tree down with the ax. To cut the tree down, she must move far away; that is why her body is like that, far away. Her body is moving from the tree. Her arms are longer than her entire body; the woman cannot lift them. She cannot move. She knows about the ax, which is in the air, higher than her head, higher than she can reach. The ax is now falling through the arms of the woman. Nonceba moves her arms forward to protect the woman, to remove the ax from her hands. Nonceba's arms are tied to the bed, so she cannot move. She has to watch and be silent. She can only see. She cannot say a word. Not a word. She cannot speak. Not a word.

The woman is now standing in a pool of blood. The ax has disappeared. She is no longer trying to lift her arms. She is not part of it. Not part of it at all.

A bandage goes round Nonceba's head, round and round and round. A hand is moving over her eyes, a very careful and small hand. "Is this too tight," the voice says. It is not a

question. It is only a statement. It is a touch. Nonceba can
only nod her head. She can feel the cloth pressing down, the
smell of a medicated ointment. Her mouth is slightly open
under the cloth. Her tongue is moving in her mouth. She is
thirsty; her throat is burning. She moves her tongue over and
over, searching for saliva. She wants to reach the bandage
with her tongue. To loosen it. To breathe through her mouth,
not her nose. She is hazy, befuddled, and dazed from medica-
tion. She sees two shapes out of every object—a dark part of
the shadow and a lighter part. Her world is superimposed.
When she hears the woman's voice in the corridor, she hears
her own voice beside it.

She is alone now, looking out through the window. Everything is gone. She is without shelter. Everything is changing. She has a desperate feeling that everything has already
changed, gone, not to be recovered. Nothing can be the same.
Her own arms have changed, her body. Kezi, her place of birth,
is no longer her own. She remembers Kezi, surrounded by the
hills. She has loved every particle of earth there, the people,
the animals, the land. The sky above her is now different;
a sky should carry dreams. The things she remembers have
changed: the nature and measure of pain, of joy. She was safe
before now, safe because she remembered different things,
remembered them differently, without her heart pounding,
blinding her. No one had died in her presence and made such
an absolute claim on her memory; she had not been involved;
her voice had not yet called out to the dead. Now she is in an
abysmal place, inert, held down. She is mute. A voice dying.
Unable to shape words into language, to breathe freely. She
will have to find the sources of sound inside her, a pure and
timeless sound. Then she will open her mouth and let the sound
free. Words will flow, then language. Only then will she dis-

cover a world in contrast to her predicament. She will restore her own mind, healing it in segments, in sound.

She thinks of the language of animals, which has no words but memory.

The movement of their bodies, the memory in their bones, of the places they have been. When they have tragic encounters, how do they survive? Do they close their eyes and dream, or do they dream with their eyes open? Do they dream at all? Are they reborn in sound? Do they nurture death inside their bodies like a hurricane, their tongues inaudible? She would like to know the language of all wounded beings. Where do they begin when everything is ended? Is there a language in the ending of the mind, of all minds? She shakes her head from side to side, slowly, suffocating, feeling the insupportable anguish that will soon overtake her, that has been with her each time she has opened her eyes and known she is awake, alive. Before this, she knew how to hold a thought in her mind. Now she is vanquished. She makes no claim to living, to her own survival. Now she is afraid to look away from the red flowers outside the window; she is grateful for their presence, a shape, a form for her mind to absorb, to memorize. An object, distinct, for her senses, with color and no sound. It is better to look at the flowers than to let a thought shape, settle, find a comfortable spot in her mind, where everything has been spilled out like water, emptied, where the sky has changed permanently, the names of things vanished. Everything has changed, and changed her way of seeing, of inhabiting her own body, of being alive. There had always been two of them, one walking beside the other like a shadow; now she is alone, the shadow to her own being. The other is vanished with a sudden and astonishing finality.

A man is approaching from behind the hibiscus bush. He removes his hat as he reaches the ramp. The hat folds into his hand. He disappears behind the door, hidden from her eyes. He has moved past the entrance, into the hospital building. Nonceba continues staring at the empty space the man has occupied. She can see him again without closing her eyes. His hand moves to his hat; he removes it, folds it just when he has gone past the hibiscus bush. She sees him framed by the red petals. She keeps his face there, among the petals, his head bowed, the arm reaching for the hat, then coming down. She sees only the side of his lean face shaped among the blooms, framed by red petals. He wears a black jacket, a white shirt. When he enters the building, she sees his back, his head without the hat, the doors without him, her mind without the view of him, empty. Then she brings her eyes back to the flowers, where he is not. Only the flowers. They have large petals. Footsteps interrupt her thought, confuse the image in her mind. The man disappears in ripples, as though her mind is a pool of water, and something heavier than he has fallen in and made his image ripple. The footsteps are again in the corridor. The voice is near, nearer than the petals she has to turn to. Someone speaks to her there, beside her bed. She sees him. Who is this man standing beside the bed? She would rather be alone. She looks closely at him. He has put his hat on the chair. He touches her forehead. She does not know him. She had watched him through the window, and now he has grown out of her mind into the space next to her bed, speaking to her. In this manner, she recognizes him. He has walked through the door, past the flowers outside. A shape. A man outside a window. He does not say who he is. She does not listen to his lips, moving, speaking. She turns away, straining hard, needing to say something that will send him away. Nonceba shakes her head sideways. Faster and faster. She closes her eyes tightly and shakes her head again. Vigorously. His touch. He must not touch her. The hand pulls away.

She turns her face toward the man speaking. She would rather be alone, so that she can sleep. She feels angry with this stranger for making her feel helpless. Without words, she cannot make him move away. She is trapped by her silence. There is a chair. The man sits in the room all day. He shifts in his chair often. She can hear his jacket making a soft sound, of fabric sliding over fabric, the cloth of his trousers when he places one leg above another, and changes shape. Otherwise, he says nothing else. He does not come near her again. He watches her from a distance. She watches the hibiscus all afternoon. If she turns her head from the hibiscus, she encounters the man. His job, perhaps, is to sit and watch her. Nonceba opens her eyes and looks steadily at the hibiscus.

She has never felt more strongly about her choice against red blooms.

"Look!" Thenjiwe says. "I have picked the most beautiful flowers for you." Thenjiwe has brought the white flowers from the riverbank, they have double petals and one bloom can cover her whole hand. Whenever Nonceba imagines flowers, she sees only these white double blooms growing along the Kwakhe River after the first rains, at the end of the year. If the rains are late and the flowers are not there, then it has not been a good year, Nonceba can only sit and recall all the events that have caused the flowers not to appear.

Thenjiwe has placed two blooms in a cup in a corner of the room, near the window, so the light falls easily on them. Nonceba cannot understand why she feels sad when Thenjiwe has just given her the most beautiful flowers she can imagine. Thenjiwe is crying, and this, too, is odd. Thenjiwe never cries. Not even when their father dies. Thenjiwe is silent as they bury him. Nonceba can still feel the sun on her forehead. They have been standing in the sun for a very long time.

"Tears are for joy," Thenjiwe says. "Not sadness." Nonceba walks into the room, very angry, and closes the door behind her. How can Thenjiwe say such things about their father? Their father, who has died. Then the door opens. Thenjiwe follows her into the bedroom. She sits on one end of the bed, nearest to the door. She rises and tucks the bedspread in, gathering it into pleats, neatly inserting the clean folds between the mattress and the wooden base, as though this were an ordinary day, and bedspreads have to be tidy. Their father has been buried. Why should any of them care about bedspreads? Nonceba wonders. Thenjiwe finishes her task and returns to her place above the neatly tucked corner of the bed. The rest of the bed is against the wall; the other has Nonceba sitting on it, obviously not willing to move. Underneath the bedspread is a striped blanket, green and white.

"When true sadness enters your heart, Nonceba, it is like a piece of the sun. A fire burns everything. A fire burns water. I have a piece of this sun lodged inside me today," Thenjiwe says. She leaves the room without saying anything else, and Nonceba continues to sit, to think of the sun up in the sky till her eyes are burning, once more, with tears, but she must stop and listen to Thenjiwe. She sees the daylight filling the room and knows that this is the sun; this smooth light has brought the sun right into the room. If she follows a single ray of light, she will arrive at the sun. Nonceba bends down and slowly starts to tuck her side of the bed. She does this so slowly that her arms ache with the agonizing movement of it, for it is only a little task, but she would like to spend the rest of her life folding away, placing this simple neatness into her mind. Tidying her mind.

One day, she is wheeled into a room in which there are rows of beds. It is a different place in the hospital, a less private ward. Nonceba feels bare, exposed. She has to deal with other people, looking, watching, turning their bodies toward her, wondering about her. She can hear many different voices all around her before she notices that no one is awake; these are the murmurs of those who sleep in pain, with wounds that no one can heal; the wounds are in their hearts. These are the wounds of war, which no one can heal; bandages and stitches cannot restore a human being with a memory intact and true inside the bone. Only the skin heals. At first, she is frightened of this change and longs to be returned to the room in which she has been kept before, alone, where she could look outside, at the daylight, and nurture her own calm. Her arms are now free. She can move her arms if she wants to, but she does not; she keeps them close to her body. She can rise from the bed. She can walk about. She can find a mirror. However, Nonceba keeps her entire body in one position. She is too frightened to move her arms. Everyone in this dormitory is bandaged, at least as far as she can see without lifting her neck and raising herself off the bed: damaged.

She searches for the woman whose voice has long been with her. She, too, is here. Nonceba would like to approach each bed and ask for her, but she knows this is futile, an impossible search, to follow a voice to its source. She would not know what to ask, how to ask. She is chasing shadows. To speak to the dead, one must assume a silence to exceed their own. She has no doubt that the woman she had listened to has died in the middle of her weeping. She can only listen till she hears that voice rise again. When she hears it, she will raise her head from the pillow and look at the woman. After deciding on finding this woman, Nonceba feels better about being in the dormitory. She must maintain a deep silence, in

which she can hear every sound. She will separate all the murmurs, the mumbled words, and find the ache in that single
voice that she remembers. She has a purpose now, in the long
dormitory, to fill the many hours when she can no longer turn
and watch the hibiscus bloom. In this dormitory, she faces a
long blank wall, white, along which are many beds. The windows are high up, beyond reach, above the beds and behind
her. Finding this woman would be like finding a piece of the
sun lodged in her heart.

Nonceba sees Thenjiwe's face lift upward, not with joy,
even though the sky is bright and blue. Thenjiwe thinks she is
alone in her pain, but she, Nonceba, knows how to follow
Thenjiwe all the way to the sky, beyond life. Nothing can separate them from each other. She is whispering to Thenjiwe,
waking her, telling her that she is not alone; they have died
together; they are sisters. Nonceba shakes Thenjiwe's silent
shoulders but fails to bring her back from the depth of that
devastating silence; neither of them has lived, survived the
other. "To fly, first you close your eyes in daylight, like this."
Thenjiwe covers Nonceba's eyes with her palms. "Can you
see anything now?" she asks. Nonceba places her hands over
Thenjiwe's arms, which are resting over her shoulders, and
they stand close together. Nonceba would like Thenjiwe to
remain as close to her as this, surrounding her with her voice.
It is dark and warm under those hands resting on her face.
She is starting to laugh again, like Thenjiwe.

If you close your eyes in daylight, you can only open them in
darkness. Nonceba wishes to tell Thenjiwe this truth, which she
has discovered with her own body. With her entire body.

Independence is the compromise to which I could not belong. I am a man who is set free, Sibaso, one who remembers harm. They remember nothing. They never speak of it now; at least I do not hear of it. They do not state that we gathered handfuls of honey, each of us. We placed our arms among bees. These scarred hands, the flesh missing, are scented hands. An inch burned from every finger. The smallest of my fingers no longer bends. Something went quiet inside my head. I heard it stop like a small wind. First, my entire left arm stopped moving, or moved but I did not feel it—it dangled. I moved my right hand. I held my left arm in my right hand like something I had picked from the ground, a discarded object. The numbness spread. I moved the arm up and down not knowing what to feel, wondering how I would survive the hills of Gulati, wishing the arm would just drop off, rather than hang loosely like that. It may even begin to rot, I had no idea. If it did, I would be eaten alive by vultures. I bit my thumb and felt nothing. I bit hard and reached the bone. This is how I lost the flesh there. I wanted to reach something, to restore feeling. A nerve had vanished.

On my hands are the perfumes of fires that we set alight by striking our fingers on dry rock, in Gulati. Rock stretched for miles with nothing above it, seamed with the blue sky. Impervious. From this rose our restless fires, which we did not allow to flame beyond the height of the rounded bone on our ankles; we cupped our hands over them; to hide a fire with your body, this is the most difficult task of all. Skin burns like dry leaves, then hardens like an exfoliated thing. When a body heals, then you discover that a body is made of layers of skin; even the human mind is like this, willing to be unclothed several times, to be naked over and over, healing in patterns like a wound, in scales. Look at the tips of my fingers. These are the fires of Gulati; these are the scars of Gulati. A man lit a fire with his own fingers and survived. He knew the smell of his own skin like a fragrance. The skin burned before he had lit a flame. He was already dead, an exhumed thing breathing. His arms a nest for a continent, a battlefield.

In Gulati, we planted land mines in shrines, among absent worshipers. We called out our own names among ancient shadows, the rocks that watch over you all night while you sleep. One rock is pinned on another, and another, smaller, suddenly larger than the eye can see, past trees, past the steady flight of birds; the entire formation is suspended in the sky, shaped in a balanced symmetry. We wove through leaf and thorn toward each mysterious image. At night, the rocks held shadows from the moon, which fell through trees whose branches were free of leaves. The stars spread over the rocks and lay there till we tried to touch them; then they vanished, as though they had sunk deep into the rock, their light lost to our eyes, to our touch. The stars dart like night insects, like torches handheld.

If you lie flat over the rock and there is no moon, the stars spread over your body like a glittering mat, and warm you like a blanket. You have the feeling of being divine. Here you are safe, part of the elements, precious, priceless like eternal things. You are fundamental, like lightning. Days go by that are ethereal like this, and you forget you are in battle against anything more substantial than time. You linger in this moment the way one lingers in a sweet memory, returning each day to the celestial contour of the rock as to a passionate lover, equally unclothed, taking the same amount of risk with your mind, alert to betrayal but not safe from harm, gaining a foolish courage with each encounter. Then the moon returns its luminous presence, and once more you regain a profile; the moon a metamorphosis, you become a target, a definite enemy. You are aware of your responsibility, the commitment in your bones to end other lives so that yours may begin. If you are fortunate, you will forget quickly that you made any kind of resolve. You are here—that is all—your arm folded over a warm rock like a hearth, your knees trembling quietly.

You are learning to resist the slow pursuit of memories. It destroys your instinct. You are learning not to thrill at a firefly, your emotion taut like a string. After all, you are being followed. It is a mistake to be static, to start identifying plants. That one, which lets out spit from its stamen in order to trap bees and butterflies. You begin to recognize its special pollen on bees, on your skin a bouquet. You are now sedentary, knowing too that plant which is a parasite, which grows on the shoulder of a tree where dead leaves and soil have gathered; it has bloomed. How long have you remained here in order to watch a parasite bloom? The other plant, whose succulence is richest at night, when you can peel its skin away with your nails, it slides off, soft, as though blanched. Too long, to have discovered this, how many nights?

You lie under the stars and recall the odor from a dead man. It is the easiest odor to return to the senses; its impurity rises from within, like a shroud. You leave your shelter of stars; after all, everywhere there are stars.

There is a shrine in Gulati where we met, about thirty of us each time. It was the only time you lay so close to another's fear. A cave called Mbelele. An enclosure, enormous, known throughout Gulati as the most sacred of sacred places. Not visited. The villagers would never enter it, not even to find a lost child. It has light in it that slides round the overhanging rock, the rock that keeps the rain out, the rain that heals. The light sparkles like water. When you feel it on your skin, you know this light has been living here for weeks: a closed place. To go in, you climb onto its back, hanging on to each groove as you ascend; each missing crust on its back is a salvation, a foothold on time. At the top is a slim aperture. You place your hand on the edge of one wall, and slide down, your legs going in first, searching the cold air. You let go of the wall, your breath rising like a swimmer. You keep falling. You are through, landed, surrounded by a fuming light. You are water and air.

From this handful of light, plants grow, burrowing deep into the floor of this cave, finding water. These plants lack any direct light; they breathe what is scattered in it. Often the ground decays, the plants dead from the stillness in the air. Mbelele has its own seasons. Closed, sound does not travel out of it. We were safe in that immobile air. We heard nothing outside our own suppressed voices; we were not heard. We left our ammunition here, and clothing, and returned after months of fighting; this womb. Long ago, humans lived here. This was clear. We found an unbroken pot and used it for our own cooking. We found a man long dead. His bones. His hair. And all over the inside of these walls of Mbelele was a thundering testimony of a sorrow to rival our own. We were perplexed. Unsafe. In our war dance. Our sure guns. Grenades. Land mines. Wounds: purple burns drying in spoonfuls of gentian violet. Our wisdom: a gauze.

To get to Mbelele, you walk through forests of tall grass, heavy-winged. During the rains, the grass is wet and slippery; the mushrooms and snails crush underfoot, the millipede, the hawk spread out, the birds feeding their young with worms; then the smell of yellow grass sweeps over the knees.

The yellow grass. We had no name for that grass which flowers in thousands under your foot, that has a fiery odor like abandoned memories. This odor floods all the way up to the hills. If you stay in that field long enough, you soon hear the bees singing, your eyelids fall, the odor pursues, and you are anointed.

The yellow grass field is not a place to linger. Instead, you hold your breath and move quickly. You move your limbs swiftly, with hardly any air reaching your nostrils. You hold your breath till your senses are alight, till your feet have acquired their own judgment of distance and safety. You are dead except for your body pulling forward. You are breathing only that air which is already trapped inside your body, nothing else. You do not breathe out. It is hard, but you get it right after a while. Then your arms are the air you long for, and you are in full flight like an eagle. You are racing forward, your knees parting the grass and opening a path for your body to slip through. You are gliding, incandescent, like a waterfall.

With relief, you overcome this field of yellow grass. You let go. You are dizzy with the force of air pounding down to your lungs. You keel over, rise quickly, mutter a word. You do not stop till you reach that ancient parting in the rocks, the valley with the stream wedged in it, which they call Simude. It glitters. Now you are close to the largest rocks of Gulati, which spill into the clouds, and the water at last is pure. It is so pure that you can hardly see your own reflection in it. A strange sensation of being invisible grips you as you look down into the water. Your instinct is to place your cupped hand into this clarity and drink, but if you do, then your body will give up; you cannot move on, not today. It is best to leave this pleasure behind—you leap over this stream. Now you have left Simude, many distances back. You are near the shrines, among those rocks in Gulati, which change shape as you approach, which shrink and expand according to the beating of your heart, the hills, which sway, which balance one above the other. When your breath returns, cools, and your eyes are open wide, then the rocks also are stilled; their shapes emerge from the distance and you realize that you are among the rocks. Among the rocks. Hidden. Everything is infinite; it is there, not you. The rocks continue in their immortal strength. You are separate. Transient. Human strength rises and wanes. Even at its summit, our strength is not rock: igneous. The mind is perishable. Memory lingers, somewhere, in fragments. Such rocks; something happened, an event cataclysmic. Something happened; this is memory. You are alive; this, too, is memory. You allow sleep to cleanse your body like warm water, like that clarity of Simude. You laugh in your dream; you rest. A cleavage in this rock. You are safe. Now. The yellow grass is wrapped over your body, the odor severe, like a carcass, dead things.

Before the rocks, among the short bushes, there is a plant, round, with orange petals, scattered everywhere and growing wild, all over that old ground. These are shelters on which many insects are born. You wake in a cloudburst. It is raining in Gulati. You are amphibious. The rain soaks you clean. Petals float to shore; humans grow wings and take flight like birds. You sleep once more.

The safest dwelling place is the bomb crater, which death has already visited. The smooth places and the flat ground fertile with insect life and growing plants are unsafe, like the unsteady rocks, unsafe. You cannot hide near a rock. You enter it; you hide inside, in its largest cavity. A room in a rock, where you may swing your arms, where leopards give birth. Your eyes sweep over the coarse-grained surface—you are alone, a carcass immured. On the rounded roof, an arm is spread to the sun. The buffalo dance.

I place my hand on the rocks, where antelopes and long-breasted women stand together. Tall women bend like tightened bows beneath a stampede of buffalo, while the rest spread their legs outward to the sun. Even now, as I speak, they are there hunting something else beyond the buffalo, something eternal. What is it that they hunt? They move past the lonely herds. Are their arrows raised against time, these keepers of time? Beyond the rock, there is nothing but light. The women raise their arms against the light. Perhaps their arms welcome the light falling from the curve of the rock, a light indelible; each stroke carries a thousand years of disbelief.

Disembodied beings. Their legs branch from their bodies like roots. The women float, moving away from the stone. Their thighs are empty, too fragile, too thin to have already carried a child. They are the virgins who walk into their own graves before the burial of a king. They die untouched. Their ecstasy is in the afterlife. Is this a suicide or a sacrifice, or both? Suicide, a willing, but surely a private matter? Sacrifice means the loss of life, of lives, so that one life may be saved. The life of rulers is served, not saved. This, suicide. The female figures painted on this rock, the virgins, form a circle near the burial site, waiting for the ceremonies of their own burial. Here, the rock is almost pure. The knees have been eaten by time; the ink is blotted out. Something is hidden: The legs are wavering strokes of blood-lit tendrils on the rock. Far from that alarming grace of the arms, the face raised high from the shoulders. Down, below the waist, the light washes over them. Perhaps they have been saved from life's embrace. Not dead. I place my hand over the waist of the tall woman, on an inch of bone, yet forty thousand years gather in my memory like a wild wind.

It is true: everything in Gulati rots except the rocks. On the rocks, history is steady; it cannot be tilted forward or backward. It is not a refrain. History fades into the chaos of the hills, but it does not vanish. In Gulati, I travel four hundred years, then ten thousand years, twenty more. The rocks split open, time shifts, and I confess that I am among the travelers who steal shelter from the dead.

I open my palm against the belly of the woman on the rock, the one with outstretched arms. The space between her knees, shafts of light. The stretch of her arm, a tattoo.

There is water here before the rainy season. The rocks split open and let the water run down to the valley to feed the animals. Before any storm occurs, something here drowns. Sometimes it is only a word that drowns.

Both the people and the animals eat the marula; they thrive on its liquid flavor. In all the ages, five thousand years ago, two thousand, four hundred years, and yesterday, the rain dancers throw water into the air, upward, past the hills, like pebbles. The water is carried in wooden plates. This is a winnowing dance: that which is raised to the sky is hope; that which is left behind can only bring death.

The crater. I trace my way back to the explosion. I feel the air for its unnatural flavors. I distill the air. I find the unholy ingredient in it. I find its man-made chemistry. I follow that smell like a wise dog. I meet limbs discarded, the flesh hanging from uprooted trees. The broken ground, an aftermath of ambush. This is my life's basin. This is the afterbirth of war, its umbilical presence. This crater is a burial ground, a mound for the dying. This is the last gasp of war. I am safe. The ground is warm. I rest in that new detonation. The odor of the dead protects me from wild animals, from hyenas, from concession-seekers. I lie among the arms, legs, the torso of an already-forgotten man. This is a resting place, this singed place, this shrine of powdered stars. I enter the lives of the dead.

The soil is chaos and ash. I enter into its burning. The soil is warm like a liquid. I am among the dead voices. I inhale their last breath. I share their last memory, this sight of thundering perfume. I hear their last sounds, charred voices. A man can vanish in a single sigh. An instant is eternal; in it, a man becomes all sound, then perishes into ash; the echo of his own death outlives him. His life cracks like bone, melts, condenses into a fine paste. No struggle can restore a man's life. Nothing can recapture his presence. He is flame, the smooth heat found on a piece of frayed metal, the mound cooling, finally silent, as though nothing sudden had happened. It is a peaceful calm, except for the signs of death everywhere, the absolute detonation. His life is past. It is not clear if he has died alone or with another. Was he alone? Was he?

I am among the dead voices. I discover a whole side of a trouser leg that is intact. It has been burned all around the edges, mapped. No loose threads—the fabric is heavy. Camouflage. No hem. No waist. The cloth starts halfway down the thigh. He was a tall man. A pocket on it. Intact. Buttoned up with metal hooks. Safe. Inside is a blue whistle. A chain on the whistle. I rest it on my palm. I close my fingers over it, fingers that are burned. I am curious. I raise it to my tongue. When my lips reach its flat tip and I clasp it with my mouth, I know that I have tasted the presence of a dead man.

I breathe in his passageway, my breath following his. I blow slowly. The sound emerging is his voice, calling from the ashes. I raise his lips to mine. An eerie passage. Not a lament, but an embrace. Not an embrace, but acceptance. The whistle has the shape of a snail. The sound from it is sharp, contained; it can be directed across distances. Sound is precise, cannot be duplicated; yet, a man imitates the man before him, with all his weaknesses. I hold the whistle with my thumb and forefinger. This is how he must have held it, the man before me. I know I have erased his last touch, the impress of his fingers. I have lost him. I blow a soft tune, which I can hardly hear. It is the only way to bury man—with a sound lighter than his own ashes.

I slide the whistle into the pocket on my right thigh. I nestle into the warm soil, as close to the dead as I can travel, as far away from the claims of the living, far from myself. Here, in this soil, there is something I can trust, someone. Everything I fear has already happened. I do not fear what has already happened—not the ungraceful arm of history, not recent and touchable deaths. Geographies are my only matter, my absolute concern. *Umhlaba.* This earth. The darkness falls close to my skin, like skin. In the darkness, a wind builds, whipping through the trees. It moves against my cheek and throws wild dust into my eyes, hard and sharp grains like bits of ground bone. If I close my eyes, I can tolerate this rough exposure; it is a merciful burial. I raise my hand to protect my face. My eyes are open to the breath of a wind. I hold the rough grains between my fingers. The sensation is not unpleasant. I sleep.

10

It is no longer a touch tracing my chin, not only a touch on my lower lip, his roughness invading, the agony prolonged, but more than that. I feel, now, each moment. I am trapped in my bones. He is here. Sibaso. In my bones.

At first, the moment is painless and I do not react, knowing nothing; then a piercing pain expands, and my body turns numb, motionless, with a searing pain. He has sought my face. Held it. His fingers, the gap between my eyes, the length of my brow, the spread of my cheekbones, my lips, moving or silent. He cut. Smoothly and quickly. Each part memorized; my dark blood, my voice vanishing. My mouth, a wound. My mouth severed, torn, pulled apart. A final cut, not slow, skillfully quick; the memory of it is the blood in my bones.

He lifts me from the ground. He holds me up, lifts me through my arm, my cracking bone. I close my eyes and find in my body a sound surrounding me, my heart hammering against my chest, sudden, my outtake of breath. I lift from the ground. Blood rushes to my ears.

His hand is on my shoulder. I press upon the ground with my hand, my wrist bending, my open palm. My arm grazes over the ground as he drags me up, and pulls, and flings me forward into his body. Wings open and flap overhead, a bird in the sky.

Human voices are far away, too far away. No one can hear. No one sees. The grass thatch of the huts, brown, spreading out, and the huts flatten and melt into gray earth. There, the flank of a boulder, dark, as though water has been poured over it. This vision leaps into my eyes, familiar, yet distant, too far, farther than my own silence. He moves closer. I hear the sound of his shoe. He is closer than that. He swivels my weight in his arms and pulls me up to his shoulder. My arms rest against his shirt. My blouse is pulled up where he holds me tightly against himself. The waistband of my skirt is loose. I feel the cloth slide down my thighs. His shirt, with the blood soaked in it, is so close I can smell it.

I know his name. I cannot call his name. My tongue is silent, his name on it. I could call out his name. I try, but I hear him breathing, near. I am standing, raised up, as high as his shoulder, pulled up. Himself poised for another action. His mind is reeling. I know he will kill me. I close my mind as simply as I would close my eyes, effortlessly. I have been waiting; he, too, has waited, thought out his action, calculated his own capacity to inflict harm. His eyes are everywhere. This I see. I close my eyes briefly. Perhaps I do not close my eyes at all, but I miss his next act. It occurs between one breath and the next, one gesture, one act. I carry this moment now like a blindness.

His movements are quick. I do not remember when or how anything occurs, the unfolding of his fierce act. I search and search for the precise moment of his action. I do not find it. I have been waiting, alert to each of his movements. There is a blank moment when I miss all the motions of his body, the ripple of his mind. There is a moment when I lose his one hand under my arm. His scent vanishes. His brow. He pushes my head forward—this I remember—and his hand locks over the back of my neck. Briefly. He releases my face and both his hands are before me. This I miss. I am still. I do not remember where the palm of his hand is, but it is no longer on my neck, no longer behind my body, but in front of me. I do not remember any of his actions without feeling him pressed on my body, following his body like a shadow, tracing the outline of his mind. His arm swings. Moves upward. Is swift and quiet. I am on the ground once more. I miss his arm swinging toward me, and him, holding the shape, the curve of my body on his palm, on the edge of his sudden and fine instrument. I recall no sound. I hear nothing. Not a single intake of breath, his or mine. His face so silent, I do not feel his first stroke. It falls on my flesh like light on water. Soundlessly. Like a sharp and burning light.

I fall in a spiral. The ground comes toward me. I am on the ground, my ribs pressed down; my head is throbbing. I feel my blood slide over my arm, my face down, over my arm, sliding with blood. I am alive: I will bury my sister with my own hands. I will live. I crawl. I look for Thenjiwe. I scramble across the ground. My mind tosses, reaches, touches something solid outside my own body. I pull my arms apart, and stretch them as far as I can reach. I find the shocking stillness of her shoulders. The softness of her body, which is soon dark under my fingers. Everything darkens. I see nothing more. I do not hear my body sink to the ground, buried in that bottomless silence.

Later. I hear voices surrounding me. There are movements everywhere. I feel the ground pounding. Then I am being lifted from the ground by a voice weeping. A voice splits the air, so close that it seems to emerge from my own body.

The voice is that of my father's eldest sister, Sihle, who lives not too far from our own homestead, in my grandfather's kraal. Sihle's voice rustles like leaves; it is so low that she searches for every word. Feeling that whatever she has said has not been heard, she repeats a word, then another, stammers, grasps.

Everyone calls her Sihle, even though all the mothers in Kezi are called by the names of their children, especially if these children are sons. She lives with her four children— Samkelo, Zenzo, Bongani, and Nkosana. Her eldest, Samkelo, even has a wife and his own small daughter, Thandolwenkosi. When my father was still living, he called my aunt by the name of her first son, Zenzo, only when he was chastising her, telling her not to answer back or telling her to take her foolishness away from his daughters. Thenjiwe and I both loved her. So did my father. We slip out of Father's brick house to her warm embers as often as we can. At night, we wrap our shoulders in moonlight and take the winding path to her hut; the crickets sing beneath our feet; the tree is shaped like a woman dancing. We are not afraid. We know no harm and lie on the mat near the hearth till morning. And laugh till we have swallowed all the smoke from Sihle's fires. She has the tiniest voice possible, and we listen carefully whenever she talks. We halt our own restless voices. There is silence and speech, fall and rise, whenever Sihle is about. There is a steady rhythm. The silence marks the times when Sihle talks and gives us our histories, like treasures. We hold our voices still, eager for our pasts, for our futures. When there is no light, our dreams emerge out of a thick darkness that we can gather with our arms.

Sihle is not married to Ndabenhle Dlodlo, the man with whom she has had her four sons. However, everyone in the village calls him by the name of his first son . . . sekaZenzo. In the mouths of all the people of Kezi, they are as married as if they lived together. Sihle refuses to leave the home in which she was born. She confides in Thenjiwe: "If I do not marry him, it is best. Look at your father and the grief still resting on his forehead. Your mother went back to her village because she had tired of his desire for a son. After you were born, she lived with him only another five years and then left. My brother did not remarry. Your mother took his heart with her and buried it under a rock. I do not want to have to steal a man's heart and bury it under a rock because of a desire that has decided to visit his tongue."

It is Sihle who is blamed for anything the women in the Gumede family fail to do or do improperly—talking to strangers, our inability to secure husbands, and stubbornness. Blamed by the men in our family, that is. And at such times, Sihle is referred to in the most polite terms, naZenzo. My uncle Mduduzi, my father's brother, also lives nearby. He has a voice like a whip.

I hear Sihle's voice. She is calling upon all the names of her children as though the existence of their names in our midst will attend to our desperation. She moans a lullaby that flows from the sky to the earth. She awakens all our ancestors. "Mpilo Hospital," someone says, "in the city." Voices are muddled. I hear one voice over another; words swallow words, die within words before I hear them, catch them. They slip out of my head before I have understood their source or gathered their ability to heal. Sibaso's voice is the closest. It crushes between every other word before I can hear. His voice makes every other sound perish. I cannot hear, and tremble, lost and blind to everything except his version of events, his persistent pursuit of what has happened here. His question. Frantic. It has happened. But what is it? He asks and asks. Who did this? Who? He is asking no one. None of us was there, not I, who is being carried from it, not even Thenjiwe, who has died from being here. Who?

The headmaster of Kunene Primary School is going to drive us to Bulawayo in his truck. "There is a roadblock every thirty kilometers," Sihle says. Her voice is very far away, but determined, resolute. "Will we reach Bulawayo?" she asks. "When they see us, the police will let us through," someone else responds. It is my uncle Mduduzi; his voice is sharp against all the other voices. "These roadblocks can be dangerous," Sihle whispers again, her arm under my shoulder, under my arm, holding tight. I am safe in her arms. I feel the silence of her voice. I must live. I do not want naZenzo to be blamed for my missing voice, for Thenjiwe dying.

I try to speak. I try hard to move my lips. I want to tell them everything I have seen. The water falling from the bucket that Thenjiwe was carrying. The sliding mud, red with blood. The man, Sibaso. Perhaps he lied about his name. I do not know. I want to describe him, each word he spoke, each strand of hair, his violent contempt of the living. I want to speak.

My voice is low; not even I can hear it. I fall deeper and deeper, till no voices can be heard. I cannot feel my lips moving, or find the shape of my words; a shape to match my words. My mind struggles till I am breathless and a dark pain penetrates my body, and spasms shake me to the root.

When Sibaso's voice vanishes, I know that this is worse than his voice burning over each of my nerves. I listen hard to his voice again and keep it near. I wake. I do not sleep. I hear a car moving, sliding onto the tarred road. I listen to car wheels. I breathe carefully, afraid of my own body. A radio at Thandabantu Store, the sound of a group of people talking calmly among themselves. We turn into the road and go past as their voices fade under the running wheels. First, the dirt road, then the ground is smooth, tarred. I can see the marula tree as we drive past and leave it behind us. I see it and the sky above it. The leaves are moving softly. A woman calls from one side of the road. No words on her tongue. Perhaps the beginning of a name. She calls till her voice has fallen far behind us as the car moves on. Perhaps she is only calling for her child.

Ahead of us are the mountains of Gulati. I can imagine this view as the car moves forward, though I am not looking at it; only the blue sky is brushing over my forehead, so close that I am floating through it as we move down the road, as I lie at the back of the truck, as I measure my frail memory against the movement of a car and the expanse of a horizon. Sihle has removed the scarf from her head and tied it all the way around my face, over my mouth. The cloth is wet with blood. I rest on her lap all the way to Bulawayo. Then my eyelids drop, and the darkness is comforting.

I feel the cradle of her arms, wet with blood; my temples are throbbing. "You must live," Sihle says. "Then I will show you the very rock on which you were born. Do you know that your mother gave birth to you on her way to the river? You were born suspended between water and stone. How can you be weak when you are made of the two most stubborn elements of the earth? Nonceba . . . Nonceba . . . " she calls. Sihle has a way of scolding you just to prove how much she cares, but my body is dead as we travel from Kezi through the Matopo hills, past the encircling hills of Gulati, dead. We do not see a single policeman or a soldier. None. We travel smoothly, as though this were a new day. I cannot absorb the distance we have traveled. Though I am awake, I am unconscious to the frenzied passage of time. There is a storm in my head. I reach the end of an eternal darkness. When I think of Sibaso, I feel a revulsion so deep that my body heaves forward and Sihle whispers that I should keep still. She holds my body down. I sink into the comfort of her voice, surprised to be alive, to be at the other end of this blank horror and be alive, able to open and close my eyes as though it were no great matter to open and close them, and find each time that same death flashing past my eyes, the man Sibaso majestic in his own discovery of the human heart—malevolent. I hear him throughout this journey, and underneath it all, a part of me wants to stay awake, and hear him. It is a long time before I realize that I do not need to keep on saying quietly to him, "Let me go . . . Let me go."

Nothing is said. Not about Thenjiwe. Not about the war. Nothing said can return Thenjiwe to us. Nothing said today or tomorrow. Nothing.

11

I fought in the hills of Gulati. I am a man who is reconciled. My mind is scalded and perfectly free. My mind is a ferment. What is it to live? After a certain point, reality stops coinciding with our wishes. When I was born, my mother had already died. She had stopped breathing. I swam out of her body, which flowed like a river. It is this to be alive. I am among the drowned, those with a feline imagination. How many times have I lain awake in the forest to see the sky give birth to a multitude of stars? I rest my palm open. There, in my palm, a thousand strokes of light, a thousand years. How many years, with my palm spread to the stars, before all my senses are restored? I count each nameless ancestor on my dead fingers. The one buried in a noose. Nehanda, the female one. She protects me with her bones. I embrace death, a flame.

The city. I move past the semidetached houses of my former street; two rooms for each family. I move in an unending dream. It is good that it is raining. I do not meet many people. D 43874, D 43875, D 43876, D 43877. On and on. The numbers of the houses appear in black ink under the low asbestos roofs, above each front door. The houses are painted in pale blue, a green tint, lemon yellow, peach. Each house is held together by a fence, never more than a meter high. Small

bushes are cut neatly back. A series of stones painted white—
any boundary will do. To enter each yard, there is a small
gate: the rusted old door of a car; panels of wood joined
together, shaped into a square, painted; a mesh fence twice
folded, then hooked to a metal frame. These I see from the
edge of my vision; the water is running from my forehead and
circling my eyes. It is raining. A brief rain. On my right a tree,
bright, clustered with lemons. I walk. Nothing matters. My
arms, moving in the rain.

This is independence. Arms wave through windows. Arms
voiceless, shaped behind glass. Dark branches moving. A
whirlwind. Raindrops. A window opens. A voice shouts, tearing the air like cloth. I am in Njube Township. When I raise
my arm and knock, someone else opens the door. It is a voice
I do not recognize.

"Yes. Can I help you?" he asks. I know immediately that
this house is now his.

"I am looking for my father." I give him a name: Sibaso.
He shakes his head and keeps his hand on the door handle,
from inside. He is wearing a vest and white cotton shorts. His
feet are bare.

"He does not live here. I do not know him," he says, shaking his head again as though to banish sleep from his eyes. I
look at him. He has flat, innocent eyes, and high cheekbones,
too beautiful for a man. His figure is lean. He could be thirty.
He searches my face, too.

"I was in the struggle. I have come back, with the others.
I used to live here." His face does not change. He is afraid,
perhaps.

"I do not know your father. I bought this house from
another man. A year ago. His name was different from that. He
may have known your father. But he died. He died from

malaria. He had been taken into prison. The prison said there was no quinine. No one came to claim his body; that is how I know. They found this address on him. It was said his only son was in the bush. That was why he had been detained. To answer questions. His name was different from yours. I could look it up, if you are willing to wait." He retreats into the darkness of the room. The kitchen. I used to live here. I know the house.

"That is all right. I will talk to the neighbors. Perhaps they remember him and have an address. Perhaps they remember me."

I turn away and leave. I have no intention of talking to the neighbors. Perhaps my father has changed his name, as I have. It might not be my father who died. I allow this opportunity to exist, to connect me to my past. I wonder about the new tenant, not my father. Why is this man not joining everyone on the streets? This whole street is celebrating. A thief could go and steal from every home, and no one would notice. No one is inside. There has been daily and spontaneous festivity. An individual wakes from sleep in the middle of the night, and moves from house to house, knocking on each door, announcing that independence is here. This solitary act is not only tolerated; it is emulated. To celebrate is to be joyous without measure. After all, an entire nation has sanctioned your joy, demanded it of you. Your response must be immediate; if you wait till after independence, you will dance alone in the streets. Everyone will have closed their doors and their windows, tired of celebrating.

Before my feet have moved down the last step leading from his door, the new tenant calls to me.

"Perhaps this will help. I found it in the kitchen. It was the only thing left in the house. Please take it. You may give it away afterward. It was in the house, in the kitchen. There was nothing else." He hands me a book. *Feso*, by Solomon Mutswairo. I receive it. I have read this book. I read it in my first year at university, and abandoned my studies at the end of the year. How could this book have survived all my journeys? I lift my hands, the palms held flat, the thumbs raised. He places the book between my burned forefinger and my thumbs. He stares at my hands as though understanding me for the first time. I shift the book to one hand, my left. He watches my movement the way one watches a chameleon, wondering if it will reach the next branch.

"Thank you," I say to him, while he remains glued to the door. His eyes pull away from the sun. He must have stayed in all morning. I walk away with the book in my hand and search the naked air for waving arms, for joy.

Joy: It is a task to be achieved quickly. Yet there are those, like the new tenant, with restraint. They stand in front of mirrors and seek their own truth, and wonder what the new day can possibly be about. Such a different individual will take independence as a personal matter, and stay indoors, lock his door and cover his windows with a torn cloth so that the sun can come through but no one will believe he is alive. He will hear a knock. He will open the door or leave it closed, as he chooses. I liked the new tenant; he was cynical in the midst of the loudest joy. He has failed to understand what people have been doing waving miniature flags in the air for weeks. It has made him shrink to the core, and when he saw me, perhaps he pitied my involvement. He has not adorned himself like the rest, and has shunned those who suddenly wear expensive garments all day, and go to the beer garden in nicely ironed shirts to drink Chibuku. Their women, whom they used to leave behind at home, suddenly appear pressed to their arms, wearing polyester skirts and georgette blouses, and shoes with three-inch heels and leather tops. The elaborate hairstyles of the women give the false impression that everyone has a wedding to attend.

In the middle of the street, just before reaching Njube High School, where I intend to get a bus to the city center, I decide to open the book. I search the small print on its opening pages. I feel an explosion in my head. I hold on to the fence of the school, like a prisoner. I cling tightly, my mouth dry. Held between the old pages is a folded map. Creased. There is a single arrow on it. My escape. Those many years ago. Between the map and the first page of the book, I find a crushed spider weighed down by time. This spider is stark on the print. Was the spider trapped when the pages, once opened, were suddenly closed, too quickly for its lengthy but bent legs to carry it past danger? No time for that speedy spiral upward on a single line of silver web? Spiderwebs. I have seen spiderwebs in the rain, in Gulati. There is more than one rainbow in a web. The most complex web carries many rainbows. No matter how heavy a rainbow is, it cannot break the back of a spider: A spider's web does not break. It stretches, just like time. For this spider, a rainbow has broken its web. In war, time weaves into a single thread. This thread is a bond. Not all bonds are sacred. The present is negotiable; the past, spider legs that once were needles.

I have found a spider stain beneath the aged surface of this map. A word hides under the brittle smudge where the spider sinks into the fraying paper. This paper is old, but not old enough for a spider to evolve into a different shape, to smudge the stain, like spilled tea. No. Not that old. I lift the sheet and this shape falls off the web of words, a fossil floating in noon light, perforated like a dry leaf. I wonder if spiders bleed before dying, before drying.

The crushed spider is an outline, the shape alone a faint sketch in charcoal—its skeleton raised to the surface after being crushed between pages; possible to be held between pages; cannot merge with words. Humans become fossils by being buried in stone, not by being held in air. In fire, they burn. In stone, bones are held still. Of all continents, only Africa has known the crushed solitude of a dead spider. Charcoal perfect.

I open leaf after leaf of fading ink. The paper folds lightly while the dust escapes and is caught by light. Flecks float in upward strokes of light. Spider-leg light. Time swings forward.

Unless you know too much about spiders, a dead spider crushed between paper is neither male nor female. This sort of weightlessness should be experienced at least once by each human being, and all the time by all nations.

12

D aytime is the hardest to endure. Objects are clean, as though washed, clear and distinct, submerged in light. My mind lacks an equal sharpness. There is no sure light in it. I see less. A blur in the room veils everything. Light is pure. Edges are sharp. My mind dulls everything till I swim in a vast opaque liquid. Speckles of light float in the room in which I dream while I am awake, yet not truly alive. I wake in a sweat, drenched. I wake with Thenjiwe's name held on my tongue; my mouth is filled with saliva. My limbs are stiff. No part of my body can move; my fingers, my arms, every part of my body is again still. I lie on the bed, listening to my body turning slowly into stone. My jaw is held tight. I do not shout. Then I see a figure move. I see light falling through a sieve like a soft rain. Light is sprinkled through the room. The voice approaching is clearer to me than the light.

Sihle walks into the room, toward me. She wipes my forehead with a wet cloth. She takes my stiff arms into her own. "You are safe," she whispers. I move my arms, murmuring, my mouth stiff, as though sewn up, stitched like the hem of a dress, folded; heavy with numbness. I am unable to speak, my forehead is heavy. I carry words at the back of my mind, names of things, objects, places I do not know. My entire face is swollen, and it throbs. The skin on it pulls down and tightens; then my words quickly withdraw. My mouth has no words, shriveled. The thread going in and out of me will eventually fall off. I sleep with my arms spread over Sihle's lap, with her face watching over me like a child. When I open my eyes again, it is already night.

I am alone in the room. My arms rest neatly on my sides. The skin on my mouth breaks and cracks like clay. I move a finger over the edges of my mouth. The skin peels off in small bits like a broken shell. I open and close my mouth. I suck air into my body. I move my mouth all night, in the dark. I am chewing the air. Anxiously, I test my ability to speak. I have not heard my own voice for so long. A sound moves from the bottom of my chest, rises to my throat. A grating, flaking sound, like a cough. I close my mouth, breathing deeply in, till my words dissolve. I hear my teeth touch, hit—a beat of stone. There is no light left in the room. A curtain is drawn. The darkness is a rapid chorus of crickets, shrill, piercing, strident. I would be satisfied to imitate this sound. The hissing chorus of insects, an enviable refrain.

The morning carries a sudden rushing sound like heavy rain, but this is not rain, only the frenzied winds of July, which can last an entire day without a drop of water falling from the sky. I hear the sand lift. The wind is high and turbulent and beats hard against the walls. It sweeps the dry grains of soil and hurls them onto the grass roof, beating down. The dogs bark, with their bodies flat on the ground. Their voices are thin convulsions, like my fear. Through the window I see the air darken and swirl past. The morning has lost its loose light. The wind rushes onward and branches crack. Heavy grains dash furiously against the mud walls. The wind beats over the metal frame of the empty cart that is lodged behind the hut. A silver sound, like pieces of sharp glass, as the sand hits upon metal and cuts like a knife over the edge of the cart. A boulder juts out near the field just behind the huts and the brick house, an obstacle, a high, smooth boulder of polished stone, straight, with a rounded top that stands higher than all the huts. The wind circles and whips against the rock repeatedly, sharp, grinding, unable to move or hollow the stone. I turn. A leaf is stuck against the window. Pressed down. I watch it as the wind moves about in every direction. The leaf is flattened, spread out. When it finally slides downward like a snail, the wind has also moved off. I can still hear the various sounds, the air pushing beneath the door—an enviable sound. The trees are rid of their leaves. My mind is quiet. Not rushing like the wind. Perfectly still. Like the leaf on the window, pressed down by the thoughts rushing against it. Raging against it.

13

Nineteen eighty-two. You can smell the unpicked fruit from the large marula tree for distances, past one village to the next, and another, as far around Kezi as your body can go. If you cannot catch the scent of it, for whatever reason of your own, then for sure you can hear it; it is in all the minds of the otherwise solitary and quiet inhabitants of Kezi. Fruit has been falling off the marula tree endlessly, and now the rains are near—if there are going to be rains at all, that is. Last year again, the maize crop withered and left a starved and violated population even more bewildered. There is no harvest. Now this. The marula tree has been yielding and dropping fruit nonstop since the middle of the year, and in the morning, when the air embraces the first light, simultaneous with that light and that embrace, there is the scent of a divine and almost sinful succulence. As dawn turns to day, dark to true light, the scent outpours. It flows. It wafts into a crescendo, and by noon, women are fanning themselves with mopani branches and throwing handfuls of water in the narrow spaces between their breasts. They are trying everything they can to survive the ethereal and weightless beauty of this air. The air is so sharp, you can taste it. They try everything easy and quiet, sipping water from a calabash, opening the door wider and wider to foster some sort of balance, some harmony, while the sun lowers itself slowly and shifts shadows to the other side of the huts, replicating objects that have height and distance.

Day is deep, sonorous, reverberating. By midafternoon, the body has adjusted and a few tasks can be done to their completion, though the scent is heavier, saturating the air, bathing everything in its drowsy light, a balm for the senses; eyelids close of their own volition. The ground tilts and rights itself. The ground is splashed with yellow marula. The birds swoop down into that evanescent air, spreading their wings and holding them still like fins; they land where human feet can no longer tread, then suck the juice from the splattered fruit. The sun drops over the horizon, and with an equal abruptness the scent is suspended. It vanishes, not gradually, but like a stone thrust, disappearing beneath water, instantly—till morning. The day is split into two halves: the darkness, the pure air, the craving, and then daylight, brimming with marula. Never, never has the village endured such a precise, heady, and unquenchable scent as this, not in quiet times, not during the height of the liberation war, and certainly not at independence. It is a phenomenon too tantalizing for the senses, imperfect yet wonderful. It is the only cherishable link with dawn, and they dare not cut that marula tree down for their firewood or any kind of escape; they dare not be superstitious, preferring to persevere in that profuse and dreamlike air with its promise of rescue. The marula tree. They hold on to its fecundity, and, indeed, its past memories. After all, there is nothing else left communal since the day Thandabantu Store blazed down. Kezi is a place gasping for survival—war, drought, death, and betrayals: a habitat as desolate as this is longing for the miraculous.

What is left of Thandabantu Store are the memories, now distant, though the stretch of time is brief; so much else has consumed memory, the present overwhelms the past and the future. Once, the setting of a sun engaged them and created conversation, brought comfort, light, to their faces, a dim smoothness of voices, and consolation. The herd boy, with his guide stick raised and the most sustained whistle held under a pinched lower lip, his two dogs circling and barking at the stray herd, brings the cattle to the fold. The flood of cattle goes past the Kwakhe bridge into the yellowing sun; the young boy is barefoot, quick, alert. He lags behind and picks a coin from the bus stop; his brow furrows as he tries to discover whether the face of this coin says Rhodesia or Zimbabwe. One is a relic, but with the other, he can race into Thandabantu and buy Crystal sweets before his herd is through crossing the bridge.

Part of the old Thandabantu veranda is still here, solid and undisturbed; enduring, too, is the thick, flat, low wall built around the veranda, linking pillar to pillar. Even with the dust and the rubble, the platform has the look of a surface, smooth and polished from constant use. Here female soldiers once reclined during the cease-fire; they spread curiosity and awe throughout the population of Kezi, spitting onto the ground, rubbing the smoke of fires from their eyes, bending their hips to pull to a comfortable tightness the loose shoelaces on their boots. The veranda thumps for months and months with the mighty sound of their tread, their long strides, their endless energy, their confident gazes on every curious face. They hug loaves of hot bread under their arms and step away past the huts and glide into the valley, to the Assembly Camp, which they called Sondela; under their feet is the crush of dry leaves, twigs, and insect shells.

They live in tents, thick canvases pegged to the ground on one side; on the other, a canopy is tied to the trunk of a tree. The women are said to sleep in their whole attire, in those boots—along with them are four hundred other soldiers living within the barbed-wire fence that surrounds their campground. Independence is here. Helicopters berate the air and zoom past at any time of the day. The soldiers look up and shield their eyes with their hands, which they hold still over their foreheads as if saluting. They bow under thornbushes in bloom; impervious to scratches, they draw handfuls of delicate hidden petals, throw them into the air, catch them on their hopeful upturned faces. The petals float down. They enjoy the soft feel of those petals, and passersby regard them with a puzzled silence. Walking in the grass. Walking on the Kwakhe River sand under the bridge, emerging on the other side, walking on soft sand till it reaches their ankles, and they are pulling, sinking, slipping, sinking in that deep, soft Kwakhe sand.

Each day, they wander off from the Assembly Camp back to Thandabantu, defying boundaries, banishing time and distance, avoiding the bridge and walking beside the Kwakhe River at any time they please. This veranda was their abode; they transformed it, and they became the ultimate embodiment of freedom. They made independence sudden and real, and the liberation war fought in the bush became as true as the presence of these soldiers. Freedom: a way of being, a voice, a body to behold. From this veranda, independence could be watched like a sun in the distance; an arm held up could capture a few of its rays. Female soldiers envisioning independence tuned their bodies to a slow momentum. Waiting. Here.

Today, stray paper is trapped around the raised platform, feathers, sugarcane peelings. Goats leap over the rubble of bricks and cement, the collapsed wall, the mixture of broken glass, smashed bottles, pieces of shelving, bent metal door frames, melted plastic bottles, burned wooden crates. The counter, shaped out of cement and bricks, is still standing, jutting defiantly out of the rubble. It consists of a large platform a meter wide. Here, the men who have just disembarked from the Kezi-Bulawayo bus unfold their arms. In tones secret and elated, they describe their own predictions of glory, of independence. The storekeeper, Mahlathini, keeps his hands on the till and never looks up; he laughs, but never looks up; he agrees, disagrees, and never lifts his eyebrows. He shrugs his shoulders, slips a bill into the drawer, and clamps it under the tray; he slides coins into the box. He leans back and laughs at something said. He does not want to remember who said what, and when. He does not want to know who heard him say what, and when. He picks up the murmur of voices, this tone, that intuition, the terror in the other voice. The rumor, the gossip, the number of soldiers killed, the war. Mahlathini keeps his eyes down and his fingers on the till. When the shop is finally empty, he looks up, through the doorway, and sees men lingering. He sees a woman selling baskets under the marula shade, the sun in violent waves.

At least Mahlathini lived long enough to witness the cease-fire and independence and to see city men lose their swagger and fall to their knees as the women, newly returned from the war, ease onto his veranda and call out for cigarettes in idle tones, Madison for some, Lucky Strike for others. None of them asks for Everest.

Mahlathini, long the storekeeper of Thandabantu Store, has died. Those who claim to know inch by inch what happened to Mahlathini say that plastic bags of Roller ground meal were lighted and let drop bit by bit over him till his skin peeled off from his knees to his hair, till his mind collapsed, peeled off, and he died of the pain in his own voice. He was dead by the time they tied him to a chest of drawers and poured petrol over the goods and the fabrics for sale and the body lying down— no, the bodies, for the soldiers had walked into Thandabantu toward sunset and found more than twenty local men there, and children buying candles, and the old men who should have been at that ancient Umthetho rock, dying peacefully, but preferred the hubbub at Thandabantu and therefore went there each day, all these. The soldiers shot them without preamble— they walked in and raised AK-47 rifles; every shot was fatal.

Mahlathini. They made a perverse show out of his death, accusing him of offering a meeting place where anything could be spoken, planned, and allowed to happen. He was said to be an expert at discarding the future. Mahlathini had no time to protest; neither was he invited to. The soldiers announced that they knew him, remembered him from the period of the cease-fire, when Sondela Assembly Camp was located down the valley. Did he not remember that one of the cease-fire camps was in front of his shop in 1980? Right on top of his forehead? They know every grasshopper and every blade of grass in Kezi; they know him. As far as they were concerned, there was absolutely nothing Mahlathini could add or deny about what they believed to be his current activities.

Mahlathini never looked up at the man, at the gun, at the voice. He looked down and accepted that he would never see his children again. He did not want to see who was killing him, just in case he recalled something about the eyes, the forehead, the gait of this man. He avoided encountering, right before his own eyes, that sort of betrayal. He did not want to see anything more, even if he understood this had nothing to do with memory. They were going to kill him, and said so while doing it. There was no danger of him recalling anything, of speaking against this soldier. He had a shocked and lingering fondness for independence, the many soldiers on the porch, their bodies spread like new flags under his roof.

Mahlathini's death would not be registered. There would be no memory desired of it. It was such a time, such a death. He did not challenge the accusations he knew to be false. His mind was racing like a wind past the guns and the deliberate industry of these soldiers, past the liberation war and its years and years of hope, which for him stretched first from his veranda to the hills of Gulati. Only then did the years extend to the various lands of the country, which he would not live to see or imagine, where the war, too, had been fought. His mind raced beyond the cease-fire, the grace and power of the celebrations for independence, the belief, the expectation, the ecstasy, past his own death, till his mind was no longer whirling and turning, but empty. Separate. Quiet. Dead with the agony in his body, melting. He could no longer hear the voices, the gunshots, the chaotic movements inside his store. Everything he knew to be happening seemed to take too long. What was clear and obvious was that he was not important. What was a place called Kezi compared to the charmed destinies of these men? Who was Mahlathini? He was only a storekeeper whom they could skin alive and discard.

He heard the minds of these men as they prepared to kill him. First, they shot his legs. It was when he was on the floor that they tore off his clothes and set fire to the plastic bags. They sliced and emptied container bags of maize meal from the store and used those to separate him from his skin. The soldiers slid pure through the soft mounds of white maize flour and lifeless bodies and blood. With arms powdered, with boots coated with flour, they hooked the plastic bags on metal hangers from which they had recently removed children's uniforms. They tied him up. Then they let the burning emulsion down. On him. The soldiers focused on this one activity with force and intensity, their faces expressionless as they sliced plastic after plastic, as they let the liquid flame drop, as they set the place alight, as they slid into the shoulder-high grass, the night empty of a single star. Before they had shaken off the flour from their arms, they had already forgotten Mahlathini and the pillar of flame they had left behind.

Those who witnessed the goings-on at Thandabantu on this night said Mahlathini howled like a helpless animal. When the sound died, his skin was already perforated like lace. Long before they burned the store down, he had died. What followed the series of gunshots, the torture, was a cacophony of sound, which lit the night with its explosion. The odor of charred flesh filled the air and has stayed in the minds of the Kezi villagers forever. On this night when Thandabantu was burned down, babies being weaned had to be kept longer on the breast so that their mothers could survive what had happened, aided by the warm touch of the sightless minds of their offspring. Thandabantu Store was razed, bombed to pieces, and silenced. If there are bodies under the rubble, nobody dares to approach the site, to remove each stone and broken brick and count the bones, one by one, to identify which is which; which the vertebrae that make a man stand.

Some of the men who are missing in the village are said to have certainly died there; the others, it is said, walked all the way from Kezi to Bulawayo, on that same night, having managed to escape, carrying with them the memory of a burning body and an impeccable flame, understanding more than anyone else that Kezi was to endure a time both frightful and unrefined, that whatever else was to happen would be devastating, and final. Those who had already witnessed the future found it foolhardy to stay. They were in flight from a truth they had already encountered. The team of soldiers who had congregated on Thandabantu Store had demonstrated that anything that had happened so far had not been random or unplanned. Atrocious, yes, but purposeful. They committed evil as though it were a legitimate pursuit, a ritual for their own convictions. Each move meant to shock, to cure the naïve mind. The mind not supposed to survive it, to retell it, but to perish. They flee, those men who witnessed Thandabantu burn. They flee from a pulsing in their own minds.

Others insist that nobody fled to Bulawayo on that night but that some men were forcibly taken kilometers from Kezi, dragged way past the hills of Gulati, deep into campsites where many others were being held, tortured, killed, and buried in mass graves.

The road to Kezi is now hazardous. Land mines. Roadblocks. Guns. A bus, if allowed at all to leave Bulawayo city center, is stopped and searched every five kilometers before reaching Kezi, if it reaches Kezi. The passengers are stripped naked and every item that they possess is shaken free; every pocket is searched. Those without national identity cards are asked to remain behind with the soldiers. They are marched into the forest and are swallowed by the tall elephant grass, and told to lie down till the soldiers are ready. They fall smoothly between the trees, the waving grass, in obedience. When the bus is stopped, it is unclear to the passengers who these soldiers leaping past the driver are, what their intention is—to intimidate, to kill, to extract confessions, to resurrect the dead. Kezi is surrounded by fast-paced soldiers, their minds evaporating.

14

Nonceba sees the outline of a chair beside the bed. A wardrobe submerged in a sonorous light. She wakes. The pillow is wet. A hand across her forehead. She rubs her face against the pillow. She turns over. She slips her hands under the pillow. She has been in a dream with not a ray of light in it. In this dream, she moves her hands blindly over each object; her pulse is beating against the darkness. She is standing on a high platform, her arms flung out. Below her is a garden of wildflowers. She is not dressed and shivers in the cold. She will fall naked into the field of flowers. Red.

Nonceba rises from the bed. Her legs are not steady. She pauses. A curtain lifts. Beams of light fall on the empty chair. Under the window. She rises. The bed does not creak. She is light, a feather. But she has always been thin. Like a twig, Thenjiwe would say. She must order her thoughts. She pulls down a cotton dress—calico, sleeveless. She ties the loose bands over her waist. The dress falls to her knees. The water, the mud—she must remember it all. She searches for her sandals. Someone has placed them neatly under the bed. She reaches an arm under the bed. She is strong enough, though she is dizzy, nauseous. She has to pause, and perform each of her labors carefully, turning her neck steadily. She sits on the bed and pushes her feet into the sandals, then pulls a strap across each foot and fastens it tightly. She has had a fever but managed through it. She opens the door, steps outside. She enters the air with her shoulders. The air is cold. She goes back inside the house and opens a suitcase resting beside the wardrobe. There is writing on top of it, in white paint, stating her name, Nonceba Gumede. Thenjiwe wrote that for her when she was leaving for boarding school. They would be a whole three months apart. Then the short school holidays. Then school again. The suitcase is brought out, the clothes carefully packed. She leans the lid against the wall. "Our father was the headmaster at Sobantu Primary School. Do not shame him. Do well at school; then your thoughts can be free." In the suitcase, a blue jersey—Thenjiwe's jersey. The arms are too long for her. She slides her arms in next to Thenjiwe's arms, close to her, feeling the warmth gathering to her fingers, like touch, like breathing. Blue wool, a nice pattern on the front, the wool threaded together, in and out. Nonceba moves her fingers over the soft wool. She brings the collar toward her body and breathes in, inhales, gathering light: lightness. She folds the extra length over her wrists. She slowly buttons the jersey; slowly, each movement makes her stronger. She buttons the jersey all the way down. She closes the suitcase. Nonceba Gumede. Her. And moves out of the room. Laughter fills the room. She has forgotten to pack her comb. She tells Thenjiwe. The suitcase is opened again. It is shut, then locked. Nonceba moves out of the room once more, into the unlit air, colorless. The air is still like water. It is humid. She searches the distance with her eyes. There is less sound outside than her own heart beating. The ground tilts. It shifts. She feels empty.

The mist surrounds the sky. The hills collapse. The sky is a gray-blue fluid suspended. This she welcomes, not that separate sky far away in her memory, far, deep blue, deep and blue, near, which she remembers. The mist descends over the rocks of Gulati and softens their hardness: they are pliant, malleable, insubstantial. A boulder disappears, transforms, melts. Nonceba watches as stone dissolves like salt. The rocks turn to water and sky and lift when the mist lifts, and tremble, and descend. The rocks fade off, smoothed, no longer here, not there, not dark, not present. They are gone. They have lost their weight, their heaviness. They disintegrate into the air. No longer black shadows. Not sculpted beings. Not silhouettes. They are without shape, without resemblance to solid form. No hills or rocks in the distance. They are nothing. Everything has been sucked up, swallowed, hollowed through. The mist is intense, spreading freely, pure and refined, like a powder poured down in a dazzling haze, particles suspended. Then blindness. Her eyes unseeing. Nothing between her and the horizon. Empty air. The rocks unseen. There are no words to describe their absence of form, or shape. They have ceased to be. There are no words. Nothing. There are no words to describe this lack. Suddenly, something sharp. A pinnacle. An edge emerges. In that, she perceives a drizzle of soft rain. Far away. Perhaps there is a strong wind, too. She sees gray streaks, beams of light descending, and shadow. The mist billows in her direction like a net: a transparent cloth, a shredded cloth, a laced horizon. For a brief moment, she sees a complete shape emerge. It hides. The outline of a rock meets the eye. It, too, disappears. To and from. The hills sing. This is light, piercing the horizon, molding the rocks like clay. The rocks are obedient to the light, which gives them form, shape, presence, color. They have height. They are wide. Wider. Light grows and uncovers the rocks. A mass, a conglomeration of rocks. Form and substance. Promontories. Light brushes the mist off. Mist blows off the rocks like white dust. Sharp light, straight and narrow, like shards of broken glass drifting down. Hammering the horizon. Forceful. The mist is completely gone from her eyes. A black rim emerges from the distance, quickly, harmoniously. Buried trees and rocks gain shape from the ground upward. The ground enlarges. The rocks expand. One rock rests on another, falls off another, hangs on another; one part of the rock is suspended in empty air, smoothly rounded, not falling at all. Simply waiting. Like her, Nonceba, not swaying. She is waiting calmly. Silence: a perfect dwelling place, a perfect sound to the senses. She can live off this silence from the rocks. She can feel her blood moving, thudding, from nerve to nerve, faster. She is as calm as a sentinel, watching the changes of the sky. She is alone, without a cry. Her pain is higher than the hills. This she knows. Her grief. This she accepts. The dark blue light breaks in the horizon, like a slow growth into blindness. Dark blue. When the yellow rays of the sun merge, they splash carelessly across the sky. Birds tear through the dense air, a rhapsody of wing sounds: creation occurs often and visibly.

Nonceba lifts her right arm toward her face. Gently, gently, she slides out of her sandals, walks barefoot to the house.

15

I return to the bush. I want to risk my mind, to be implicated in my own actions, having taken a personal resolve against a personal harm. Such a war. I find a prop for every truth, for every mistruth.

I reenter the curve of the hill, of the rock, of the sky. I return to the past of the hills. The earth is beneath my feet. I fall into the dry burning of wind and grass; of rock, of sky. None of them is a hibernation. I endure the war anew. I am an instrument of war. I lose all sight of pity for myself.

During the brief cease-fire, I lived with four thousand soldiers in one camp. I could tell the difference between each man, whose fear was the greatest. Four thousand soldiers with their ammunition laid down. I did not surrender. I did not fight to please another. I dug a pit and covered it with grass. I lived within it, but how long can a man be buried before he turns blind?

In the bush, I discover once more that I have no other authority above me but the naked sky. The cocoon on my fingers: death. Under my soles, ash. Nothing survives fire, not the voices of the dead. Nothing survives fire but rock.

The grass is dry and brittle. The rivers vanish; the streams are absent. A cache of arms, safe. I run till I am burning, toward Gulati, to that hiding place, the cave of Mbelele. I fall into the cave, where again the messages of the dead are brought to life with a fire from my fingers. The dry grass beats across my arms, lacerating. I run through the grass, which rises before me like a wall, obscuring the view, but I know my direction without even looking up. I can find my way. I have lived here, possessed by the hills, owning nothing but my own breath; the land is suddenly larger than the sky. I run till darkness descends and only the rushing sound of the grass beats over my skin like a vast wind; the sound as dark as the night, as solid.

Night. The air is cooler. I use it to ascend the hills. I continue till a crescent of moon emerges and gives a profile of the hills, the shape of a woman, whole, above the rocks. A still figure, a woman of stone. This rock is close to Mbelele. I know it well. Blinded by darkness, I run between the hills toward this solitary rock high in the sky. The woman stands at the top of the boulder with one flat side; above, another rock, smaller; above that, a rounded rock, large and flat—the woman of the hills. I near that rock with my knees trembling, my mind whirling, and I know that tomorrow I will vanish alone somewhere in these hills. I do not breathe. I swallow the air. I will crumble like a dry thing. I must reach that figure standing under the moon over the shrine of Mbelele, where I buried not only my weapons but a man. I buried him in water, inside the cave. He could not survive. I placed a rock above him and he lay still. The water in the caves never dries. It is as permanent as stone. My shadow falls on the grass; my body climbs rock, part stone, to find water, enough water to bury a man.

I head back to the hills of Gulati, where the caves never dry.

I, too, have come from beneath the earth, uprooted, like the rocks.

Kezi.

16

Noon. The scent of the marula fruit filters into the air, its fragrance spreading into the sparkling midday light and confusing the senses. Nonceba can raise her arm and breathe in the marula's scent, a fine layer of perfumed air over her. She inhales the tranquil and intoxicating smell of this tree, and she closes her eyes to see it, closes them enough that she can block from her mind what lies behind the tree, the remains of Thandabantu Store, which is now buried, not there, destroyed and gone. It has never been. The marula tree is alone in the clouds, high branches drooping with fruit, dangling yellow to the ground. The fruit is falling down. The skin of the fruit swells with the heat, then cracks, and the sweetness spills. Large slippery seeds hatch and slide out. The liquid flavor spreads and rises with the heat of the day, carried on the slightest breeze. The scent is everywhere, penetrating each dream, each decision. The sun is shining bright, striking pure and downward and hot enough that everyone says today it will rain, but the only thing raining down is the marula haze, coloring every dream from morning to noon to sundown.

The shade of the mphafa tree where Nonceba sits is a refreshing island of cool air; in its shelter, she feels the heat drain off instantly from her armpits and her entire body, but only the heat moves off her and not the marula flavor, which clings to her; which clings to everything; which is the air itself. From this calm shade, the eye can see some image through the heated air rising and lengthening the view of the hills, a mirage. The plowed fields stretch and cultivate the distance, waiting for absent rain, long absent, while traversing boulders and circle after circle of huts. The water is so absent you can taste drops of it on your tongue. There is no crop growing. The grass is driest, splitting and crackling, ready to burn. The grass frames the foreground of every vantage point, along pathways, dry and brown, along the roadside. The eye sweeps over the quivering grass, into which heat seeps like steam, and the viewer sways, not the grass; first that, and then the eye can rest on hill, rock, or man.

Sitting in the perfumed shadow of the mphafa tree and listening to the smooth calling of doves, Nonceba sees a man emerge in the far-distant horizon, winding purposefully along the pathway, left to right; back to the left, the pathway loops like a whip, twisting. He is coming this way. He is moving on the path that leads eventually to the house. The grass, shoulder-high for her, is only waist-high for him. He draws nearer but is still too far away; his features are blotched, a mask unmarked, dissolving. Then he is closer, and she can see him, no longer a melting shape in the sharp light, but a distinct form. Solid, continual, steady. He emerges from the lonely light. He is tall, linking rock and sky together, grass and pathway. First he has been a still point in the shimmering heat; then his body, thin as an arrow, is moving sideways, shimmering toward her, his jacket fluttering with his own motion, flapping. He is approaching her soundlessly, a man with a hat on, a man wearing a jacket in this surprising heat, holding a small leather bag over his shoulder, surrounded by a burst of hibiscus blooms. I know this man, Nonceba thinks. I know this man and that bush of hibiscus traveling beside him. The closer he gets, the easier it is to see the hibiscus, but the harder it is to keep her eyes on him, and she lets that distant heat swallow him whole. She is dealing with surprise. The hibiscus, she can see clearly, bloom and leaf, full red under the window. The top of the hibiscus tree is too high up; she cannot see it from where she is sitting, not even the sky spread out above it, which she knows is above it, far from her eyes. The man is walking past her eyes and disappearing into that place far from here, so that he is in two places all at once, and her mind whirls with its impossible thought. He is a stranger, but she has seen him before as clearly as she has seen the hibiscus, its large petals open wide and the pith of yellow inside, and the bees on it. As clearly as she has seen daylight.

Nonceba rises from the coolness into the light. Her legs can hardly support her frail weight. She is light, surprised, unsure of her own emotion, her ability to endure, to take any of her own past and hold it before her eyes in any form. She lifts her eyes to the bottom of that distance. Her heart is beating with a fear she cannot name. Far out there where an outline of him emerges, he is already taking off his hat. With a free arm, he lets his hat dangle past his knees and smooth over the grass as he passes by, slow, his movement deliberate and prolonged, intimate, pensive. Her own mind is considering each of his moves. She is absorbing each of his actions, the hat moving down and sliding over the grass, especially that. His arm is easy and free. His arm traces some movement of his mind; Nonceba absorbs each of his slow and deliberate moves. She watches his motions as though he were a bird in the sky. He has almost reached her feet when he finally looks up and meets her gaze. He is standing in front of her, with no words. It is she who has surprised him by her instant presence. He emerges from a secret place.

Nonceba has been moving toward him, without her mind choosing between moving toward him or remaining still, but the moment propels her as she tries to separate this man from the hibiscus blooms and give him a name, a voice, to reclaim him from the dizzy spell of marula and her own memory playing tricks on her. Her legs move of their own accord and she is not conscious of her own movement, simply carried by her instinct and walking in sleep. She is breathing hard as the presence of this man is separating her from the calm, cool shade and moving her into the staggering and blind light, taking away her solitude. She stands still and rests her arm on the wooden post at the entrance of the homestead, holding herself up, bewildered. She knows exactly where she has seen him, but not who he is and why he is looking downward and not up to see where he is going, rolling his hat on the grass in that feverlike air as though the world starts from his knees and then ascends, according to his will and judgment, to anywhere else. He is engrossed in his own activity, a stranger touching the dry grass with a tender stroke that moves from his mind to the motions of his arms and finally melts down to the touch of a single felt hat.

It is him for sure, but her mind contests that certainty, resists as long as possible the merciless act of being thrown violently back to any moment before the calm moment when she was resting under the mphafa tree, letting her mind just empty into the cool air around her so that she could breathe, quietly and alone. It is him now, and with him, the moment before now is him also and no longer her mind quietly handling each of her memories, unhurried. Her legs are trembling in the intense heat; after all, her body can command its own island of grief. Her tongue is dry. When he appears, randomly, all her carefully constructed peace immediately vanishes. She forgot him when she returned to Kezi after leaving the hospital bed, which of course she wanted to forget, not dwell on that memory that visits her without clarity but in a haze of days succeeding days, anger and pain, and an insistent, absolute silence. That is where he had sat watching her for a whole afternoon in her room while she looked out the window and saw the hibiscus bloom. He is here walking toward her, but at the same time she is removing him from her eyes and placing him safely away into that faraway room where he is watching her and not letting go, a room at the back of her own mind, upon which she has drawn a dark and heavy curtain, some cliff, some waterfall, and she stays safely away. He is here, and she can smell the hospital room. Between this baffling realization and attempting to catch all his movements and the details of his jacket and his height and the hibiscus bush, she is asking herself why he is here at all. Is it because he is only passing through Kezi, or is he really just looking for her, and if so, how did he know where to find her? He has ignored her indifference and followed her all the way from Bulawayo to Kezi, to this same spot on which she is standing now, watching him and wondering at his claim, but how? Who is he? How has he come from Bulawayo when the roads are blocked and a multitude of soldiers are disturbing the peace of the land? Is he a policeman, perhaps? Someone who can understand crime and criminal minds and the right punishment to mete out to a deceased past, her past; a man who can uphold what is left of the law? Is this his special pursuit? She cannot imagine why else a stranger would follow her from Bulawayo to Kezi, having waited for a whole afternoon by her hospital bed, watching her say nothing at all, unless he is on guard over some truth that he has to protect even with his own body. What else could exist as a justification for his step and stride here in Kezi and his incredible pursuit? If he had not finally spoken, if he had turned and walked back into the blistering heat, she would have believed for sure he had not been here at all, that she had dreamed him up with all the bits of memory that now lie in fragments in her mind, because that is how she lives now, with her insides all broken up; so he, too, has come together from that pile of the things that are broken up in her head and could be mismatched, any time of day, and combine to produce the most improbable event.

"My name is Cephas Dube," he says. She almost believes his presence. He is creasing his eyes against the sun. He extends an arm toward her for a greeting, his motion tentative. She turns away and walks slowly in the direction of the house, as though she has forgotten him. Leaving him behind like her own shadow. Telling herself he is not there at all. When she reaches the door, she will turn back and look again. "My name is Cephas," he says again, looking over her shoulder. He has followed her from the gate.

She is moving past the mphafa tree and can almost feel its cool shade over her shoulder, but she knows she must forget about that piece of placid earth and consider this stranger splitting her mind. She stands, waits, but not under the shade. She waits for him in the baking heat, looking away. They both pause, waiting for her to speak. She is waiting for herself to speak, knowing he is waiting, too, for he has spoken not once, but twice.

"I do not know you," she says finally, without turning to look back at him. He stays a safe distance behind her.

"I left a message for you while you were at Mpilo Hospital in Bulawayo. Did you not receive it? I left my name there."

"I do not know who you are," she insists.

Perhaps the message was received, passed on. She realizes this. Her effort has been to separate herself from her loss. She does not remember what the message said. Certainly not his name, which he now offers to her as though it should be a revelation. Perhaps his name lies unread, on a piece of paper, in the house somewhere. Unread.

"Is there somewhere we can talk? Inside the house perhaps?"

She mistrusts him, yet she responds to his request as though something in the quality of his voice makes everything all right, the most absurd action, the least considered, given the atmosphere in Kezi, and her own ordeal. Nonceba walks on silently, ahead. His voice is sincere, but should she take him into the house? She dares not take him into the house. Yet she opens the door to the main house and walks into a small room with a table and two chairs at its center. She turns back; his footsteps have ceased suddenly. He has disappeared. He has not followed her in. Had he asked to enter the house? Was that her own mind making up conversation for him? Making him real? He is only in her mind. She moves around the table and goes back to the door, anxious to find him there, real as daylight. She looks out, and almost bumps against him. He is lingering at the entrance, with the hat held in his hand, dangling it near his knees. His confidence has vanished. He seeks her absolute permission before walking in. He wants her approval.

"Do you wish me to come in?" he asks cautiously. He has sensed her distance, her distrust.

"You may come in." She turns away from him.

He enters. He pulls out a chair while she takes the tray with the candle from the table and places that on a smaller square table in a corner of the room. A basket with some dried vegetables in it, a wooden spoon—these, too, she removes. She moves all the remaining items to one side of the table. Now there is room for their voices. She looks up at him, his brow creased in concentration. Not trusting him at all, telling herself that she will accommodate him only for a while, hear him out. She is no longer frightened. He is still separated in her mind, a silent stranger sitting in the hospital room; a shadow rising from the distance up the footpath and moving toward her; a man sitting familiarly before her. Who is he?

"I remember you from the hospital," she confesses.

"I came to the hospital to visit you. I thought I could talk to you then. I tried. It was not possible. I left and decided that I would visit you here, after time had passed. I have come finally."

"Who are you?" she insists, wondering at his presence, his tenacity.

"My name is Cephas Dube. I live in Bulawayo. I have lived there for some years now. I work there."

"How did you manage to arrive here? The roads are so difficult." She waits for his answer, as though it will either raise or dispel her fear of him.

"A man I know was coming to Kezi in a truck. I asked for a lift. He was kind. He let me ride with him. We had an easy drive. He has gone on."

"You had no problems in your journey?"

"No. We had no problems."

He has not told her who the man with the car is. Why was the man prepared to come all the way to Kezi? There is nothing here anymore, not even a store. Kezi is only a place for those who were born here and have nowhere else to go. A place for the trapped. Boulders, ruins, burned villages, the dead, a naked sky. Many people have left and most of the homes are empty. He does not explain about this man, the driver who can dare that stretch of road, not as a means of escape but merely to enter this bleak wilderness, Kezi. She does not want to ask him direct questions, but the information he holds back seems crucial to her. He places his hat on the table, setting it between them. He is nervous, unable to start saying whatever it is that has led him to her. She can sense that he has something to tell her. Something important. She waits for him to speak.

"I only heard about you when you were in boarding school. Are you a teacher now?" He is looking searchingly at her.

"I was a teacher last year, but this year I am staying at home. The school has closed down. The children no longer go to school." He has not said yet who told him about her, why he had to know about her at all.

"I lived in this house once, for a few months," he says.

She looks up at him more carefully. He bears no resemblance to her uncle Mduduzi or any member of her family. She wonders if he might be a relative of her mother. She does not know any of the people from her mother's side. Everything about him is new to her; she is sure of it. Her aunt Sihle will be passing through here soon so that they can walk back together. Nonceba asked to remain behind for a short while in the afternoon, but she has lived in the village with Sihle since her return from the hospital. However, not everything has been moved from the house; this table, these chairs are yet to be moved. Strange that this man should arrive on one of the days when she has chosen to be here.

"I work in an office in the city. I file documents in an archive. One morning, I was clipping items from the newspaper. I saw a picture of Kezi in it. I read what happened to you and Thenjiwe here in Kezi. I knew immediately that I had to see you. I found out you were in the hospital. I could not believe that Thenjiwe had died till I saw you and sat within your silence for a full day. Then I believed everything that had happened. It was not important that we did not talk. It was not the best time for us to meet. I realized that I had to wait, perhaps for some months. Thenjiwe and I . . . well, we were very close once. We were with each other for a short time. It is difficult to explain; it was such a different time. Then I decided to go to the city. Had life been clearer—it is too late to think like that, but the mind wanders off, and one imagines the possibilities missed. When I read what happened to her, I could not just stay away . . . I am here now. I want to help you, if I can."

"My sister never mentioned you to me. She always told me everything in her life. Why was she silent about you?"

"Perhaps she wanted to keep this to herself, or she might not have been ready to tell you. I cannot explain it. There are matters about which someone may wish to be silent, even with those to whom one may be closest. She told me about you, however."

"No. I believe she would have told me everything. We had no secrets between us. We were very close. She might have done so, perhaps, in the future, if she had lived. If it is true, that is, she would have told me in the end," Nonceba insists.

"Loving her was like living in the stars. I wanted to marry her. We were both afraid. Impulsive, but extremely fearful. We did not know each other well enough. I should have returned sooner than I have. She has been with me all the time. We all live our lives with a foolish sense, never believing the worst that could happen to us. We may think about death, but belief is another matter entirely."

Nonceba believes but mistrusts him. He has a gentle manner, which appeals to her. He has not explained what kind of office he works in. He does not say why he is collecting information from newspapers on persons like herself. For whom is he collecting it? How would this information be used, either presently or in the future? Why had he been, on that morning, collecting information on what had been done to her, and to Thenjiwe? She has no knowledge that her name had been printed in the newspaper. Does Sihle know about it and has not told her? She resents this man for telling her about this public exposure, which she knows nothing about, for his time with Thenjiwe, which again she knows nothing about. She wonders what else is hidden. He has put her name in a file. Stored her. Pinned her down. Now he is here to find her. Determined to see her in the absence of Thenjiwe. She feels a heavy and sudden anger and wants him to leave immediately. Perhaps Thenjiwe loved him, which would mean he had been good to her, but time has passed and everyone has changed. Nonceba cannot rely on that bond he claims to have had with Thenjiwe to judge his worthiness. After all that has happened, it is hard to trust anyone; people change like chameleons. How can he come here when there is nothing here for him, not Thenjiwe, whom he claims for his own truth?

"Are you not afraid living here on your own?" he asks.

What does he know about fear, about what she has endured? What does he know besides his own intrusion? "No. I am not afraid. I grew up here. The rest of my family lives in a home nearby. If I raise my voice, all my uncles can hear me."

She sounds ridiculous, she knows, but she is reluctant to admit to him that she no longer lives here—indeed, to admit that it is because of her own fear that she has had to move. She has no wish to admit anything between them. He is right, but she has no wish to confirm his thoughts in order to make him believable; that is his task, not hers. She objects to his actions—coming to Kezi, asking questions as though he were a policeman, claiming Thenjiwe's memory in terms that she cannot even imagine.

"After what has happened here, you should be afraid. It would be wise to be afraid," he insists.

Here, he says. *Here*. Does he know exactly on which patch of ground she, Nonceba, experienced her loss? Does he know where Thenjiwe died? On which spot of ground she was killed? *Here*, he says, as though he knows exactly what happened here. He knows nothing about the here of it. The feel of that here. The sight of it. The moment so full of here. He has no memory of her here in which her sister died, not like a living thing, but trapped in the arms of a stranger. She wants to laugh, curiously and maddeningly, at his coming here and talking about Thenjiwe and saying all he has to say about his own version of events, of here. Nonceba feels removed from him, solid in her own memories. Her pain is her own, untouchable, not something to be revealed to a stranger who just happened to follow his past here. *Here*, he says, knowing nothing about it at all, the past, which has vanished. Does he not know how the ground beneath your feet can simply slide away and never come back? That here vanishes without reason and leaves you not here, but nowhere at all, and the rest of your life is this persistent loneliness eating away, and your mind is crumbling down like a wall, just like that, while you walk and wallow between the sky and the earth with no other thought but this loneliness?

"I live here. I have my wounds. I am not afraid." She rises from the chair and walks into the next room, needing desperately to be alone, away from him, but she returns quickly, wanting to speed the time between them. She has opened a window in the room.

Again she sits down across from him. She is impatient for him to leave, to stop stirring her mind like that. She sits down, wondering how long before he will raise himself up, pick up his hat from her table, and retrace his footsteps back to the main road, leaving her comfortably alone to contemplate the measureless distance between here and now.

"I think you should leave Kezi," he declares.

His voice has changed. She feels it. He is talking to her as though she is a child—his child. "I have no wish to leave Kezi. Nothing worse can happen to me now. Why should I run away? The war is everywhere. Is it not there in the city?"

"Worse things can happen if you continue to remain in Kezi, unprotected. I want you to come with me—to Bulawayo. It is not bad there. The war is mainly in the villages. I want to help you; for the sake of Thenjiwe, allow me to offer my help. I want to help. Perhaps for my own sake. Let me help. Then I will leave you alone. I know I can help you. Please let me do what I can."

The sweat hardly dry on his forehead and he is asking her to leave her home and go with him to Bulawayo. This is why he has come. He says it finally, the words tumbling, emphatic. He wants to take her with him. He insists. She feels confused by this wild expectation of his, which is based only on the intimate memory of her sister. What did they share? she wonders. What promises did they make one to the other? More than this, why has she been the outsider, knowing nothing about it all till he rose like a savior and claimed her sister and all her pain and made them his? She is both stunned and intrigued by his confidence, frustrated, angry, wanting him to move away even if for a while so that she can adjust her thoughts to the sound of his words, to his sudden presence, to Thenjiwe's secret intimacy, to her heart hammering away. How can she think about all that she has to consider while he sits and watches her and waits for her to speak? He pleads for her to agree without allowing her a moment to herself.

All her thoughts gather like dust, and through that she watches his arms resting on the table while he looks directly at her as though he has nothing to hide, and she knows that she is free to ask any questions, and he will answer her, politely and patiently. She does not know what to ask in order to clear a path between them—no, a path in her own mind. Instead, she is quiet, knowing full well that this has nothing to do with questions to be answered, but about her own intuition, her own claim to life. His request hangs over them, suspended in the room. A kindness. A request. A threat? He is waiting to be answered. Could he harm her? Is that his intention?

She had seen him at the hospital. This memory is in her mind. Were his reasons for visiting her there as direct as he now states them to have been, as kind? She knows about harm. She knows the presence of someone who will harm her—it is equally intimate. She understands how that presence can reach to the back of the mind and see right down into the pool of fear underneath. How can she listen to the outrageous proposition of a stranger who has walked up a grassy path and found her desolate heart, full with all its memories, waiting for a stranger to turn his eyes and his voice toward her and say that he is offering her life, not death? This same stranger now challenging her presence and letting her know that all she has before her is death, not life, telling her this when she already knows all about it and carries this knowledge firmly in her own eyes. Is that not what he is offering, some kind of life after everything is buried? An escape?

"Kezi is a naked cemetery," he says. "Is this not what everyone is calling Kezi, a naked cemetery where no one is buried and everyone is betrayed? There is no certainty of life, only death. To die here is to be abandoned to vultures and unknown graves. No one knows how many people have died. No one knows when it will all end, or if it will end. You cannot remain here any longer. Let me help you. You can return again if everything changes." He pleads, as though to accept his offer would be to grant him life.

She thinks of Thenjiwe and tries to link her with this man, this stranger pleading before her, offering her something akin to existence, to life. Had Thenjiwe really been with this man? She examines his face, knowing the exercise is futile but wanting to find out somehow if Thenjiwe had been with him, if he was the sort of man for Thenjiwe to like, at all, to live with, even if only for a while. She looks at his arms still resting over the table, his wrists. He has hardly moved since sitting down on that chair. He is neatly dressed, polite. Thenjiwe had been with this man, touched him. What had Thenjiwe loved about him? Was it his eyebrows, like dark ink? His voice, gentle, forceful, confident?

His kindness? His offer perhaps at all times to help, his capacity to surrender his life to others, herself, the sister? His spontaneous will? His ability to grasp another's pain? Was that it? Nonceba looks into this stranger's eyes, searching in them for the distant place where love, not hurt, begins.

Nonceba is not entirely surprised that Thenjiwe had not told her about this love and this man. The surprise is that she, Nonceba, has not found out about it before now. For if Thenjiwe had loved this man, even briefly, she had to know about it somehow, because she knew Thenjiwe so preciously, so precisely. She would have known about it but continues not to, not even while the man calling himself Cephas Dube is sitting across from her with all that love in his eyes and the elaborate claim in his mouth and not a single doubt in his eyebrows; she feels she still knows nothing about it at all, not even the first half of this tale. When was it that passion had unfolded? In which season had they loved so hidden from her, the person who knew all there was to know about Thenjiwe, including the things that Thenjiwe hardly knew about herself, which she could not express and only Nonceba could, and did, and they both accepted how necessary they were to each other?

Nonceba, who had shared a room with her sister after their mother left and commanded them to take care of each other, and they had both survived that departure because they had each other always. And then their father died, and they survived that, too, because they were adults and could survive the present even much longer than the past. And now Thenjiwe has died, and how is she, Nonceba, supposed to survive all that? Nonceba was so close to Thenjiwe, she could hear each of her dreams and tell her about them, because they dreamed the same dreams, only found different words to explain them. She knew nothing about Cephas, not this stranger with a tongue sweet like honey, saying all there was to say about Thenjiwe except the words that would bring her back, make her walk in the room and find them both with their hands on the table and their eyes staring into an absent past. None of that. Instead, a stranger is sitting in front of her and acting as though he knows all that is right and wrong for her, telling her about all her hurt and his hurt, saying Thenjiwe's name easily and without hesitation, as though he has a shape and a laugh and a personality to attach to that name as much as she does. Today, on this afternoon saturated with marula, he has just walked in and made himself at home. At home. Asking her to find a suitcase and pack her clothes, fold them, one by one, and follow him to the city, risking the battalion of soldiers rising like locusts from the bush, swarming the road, the guns slack and easy under their wrists. He wants her to leave everything, as though she does not belong here and could just leave because it makes sense to do so, makes sense to him, his view of the future and his past. Wanting to help, he says. How? To take her away. To remove her from her memories, as though that indeed could be done as easily as tossing a coin. His version of escape; her version of surrender.

Not kindness, perhaps. Something else. Then a terrible thought enters her mind and she turns from him, ashamed to think it, but she has already let it slip into her mind and has to follow that thought to the end. She has to think through that thought, then cast it aside, then keep it if need be, but she has to think it, because that is what she has to do. She has to think the worst first. Does he perhaps know who would have wanted to murder Thenjiwe and why? After all, the most unimaginable event is not only possible but probable in Kezi. As he says, it is a naked cemetery. This is what he means, surely, that there is not even a faint line between life and death in Kezi. Is he standing on that faint line? Is this his special task, to make sure that the dead cannot choose their dreams, or the living? This is what the men loose in the bush are doing and the soldiers—both equally dedicated to ending lives. Since he is a man who can take risks with tenderness, perhaps he can tell her what exactly it took for a man to look at a woman and cut her up like a piece of dry hide without asking himself a single question about his own actions, not even the time of day. What did it take for a man to possess that sort of obedience? It is in her mind, so she says it to herself, murmurs till she is satisfied, silently, accusing the stranger who is offering her a journey out of Kezi.

They are quiet for a long time, till they are both comfortable to be silent and to say nothing at all, just let the time pass. They do not speak. They say nothing, only gather their own thoughts. Finally, he takes her right hand and cradles it in his, as though he is counting each of her fragile bones. She lets him take her hand and hold it, not wanting to say anything, preferring this language of silence that they have found. He turns her hand over, holding her as if she were the most precious thought in his mind, not wanting her to leave his mind at all. He looks at her and down at her hands till she bends her fingers and folds them in his. She lets him hold her, as though she is no longer in control of her own desires, and indeed she is not. He looks up at someone else in the room, not her, as though someone else has said something and he is listening to this other voice speaking to both of them and making it unnecessary for them to say anything at all. In this long and surprising silence, Nonceba sees the longing in his eyes, the despair, old and well kept. He holds both her hands together between his own, palm to palm.

17

The sign outside the flower shop reads JOAN THE FLORIST in large silver letters. The first part, JOAN, is written in a curling, cursive print. Standing along the pavement, you can look through the glass partition into the interior of the shop. Another sign, directly on the glass door and waist-high, says CLOSED ON ACCOUNT OF THE WEATHER. However, it is sunny outside, a bright, clear day in November. On the vinyl floor, there are many different flowers contained in baskets of varying sizes, arrangements ready for delivery, some posies, nosegays, presentation bouquets encased in cellophane.

There is a door behind the low counter with its yellow Formica finish; the design on the counter is like rock, brown cracks on stone seeping into a pale yellow background. Every so often, a woman swings in from the back room with a finished arrangement of flowers, which she places gently on the floor. She wears a simple white gown and a white apron over it, and flat white shoes. She does not linger. She has a concentrated and busy demeanor, purposeful, diligent, precise. She turns and goes quickly back into the recessed room, where the flowers are being watered, prepared, cut, trimmed, pruned, then pushed and set into wire-mesh bowls, on platforms, on sponges, slid into champagne glasses and held up somehow, while others are prepared within fruit arrangements.

In the front of the shop, there are more flowers—dry flowers and silk flowers—placed on glass display stands, and potpourri, and scented soap with ribbon tied on it, and colorful floating candles, and, on another metal stand, cards for all occasions. Mostly, however, the flowers are freshly cut. When the door opens, the perfume from the mixed blooms is provocative: carnations, roses, gladioli, baby's breath. There are a few potted plants, portable, with pieces of driftwood set attractively in the basins supporting them. The glass door opens and a bell rings inside the shop; a lady at the counter looks up. The door swings back, then closes. A man is leaving the shop with an armful of roses arranged in a pyramid that touches his nose. He leans back so that he can see around the flowers and then opens the door. He rotates, clockwise. He turns his back to the door so that the flowers are safe and undisturbed on the opposite side. He moves around the door, then steps easily onto the pavement. He walks down the street with the flowers held high, higher than the approaching flow of people. The bell inside the shop rings as his figure disappears. The lady at the counter looks up. Her hair stands in neat large brunette curls, sprayed. She wears a thin pink scarf tied around her neck, held down by a metal ring over the open collar of her blouse. A thin black skirt ends at a modest length below her knees, accompanied by high-heeled sandals. Her blouse is soft, neat cotton. She is tall and wears half-rimmed spectacles, which continuously slide down her nose. With her right hand, emerald and ruby-ringed, a ballpoint pen wedged between her fingers, she slides the glasses up absentmindedly and raises her head. A thin line of red lip-stick, a face carefully powdered. Mascara. Eye shadow. She opens a receipt book and starts to write rapidly. She stops and carefully slides a blue carbon paper between the pages, then continues with her writing. A phone rings. She picks the phone up and holds it tucked under her curls. She holds it up expertly with her right shoulder, freeing her hand. She speaks and nods in agreement. She replaces the receiver. She flips the pages and moves the carbon paper. She writes. A delivery van parks in front of the shop. On the back of it is written JOAN THE FLORIST. A man gets out of the van with an empty basket and enters the shop. He limps as he walks. His body is leaning slightly to the right. He wears a white overcoat. The door swings open. The bell rings. The woman adjusts her specta-cles as she looks up.

Nonceba moves past the glass wall at Joan the Florist, walks past the shop door, which opens onto Fife Street. She crosses Ninth Avenue and goes toward the Standard Char-tered Bank, where there is a long, winding queue of people extending the length of the building. Inside the bank are recently employed black bank tellers and trainee managers newly graduated from the Economics Department of the Uni-versity of Zimbabwe. The queue from the bank stretches to Edgars Clothing Store. Unlike the Standard Bank building, which boasts stylized features and intricate architectural de-tails on its entrances and facade, Edgars is modern, all high tinted glass with imposing concrete pillars, and mannequins poised all the way around its two sides. Edgars was the first large shop in Bulawayo to use black mannequins on its win-dows soon after independence. Three years later, every pas-serby still looks through the windows at the black faces, the arms of the figures stretched out as though supporting layers and layers of cobwebs. The black customers step up to the front entrance and walk into the regulated air with a look of both pleasure and amazement.

Suddenly, the clanging of a bell fills the city avenues and streets. The sound comes straight from under the clock at City Hall, in the center of the city. Nonceba hears it again and again as it sucks the clamor of traffic and pedestrians and hooters and bicycle bells. Every fifteen minutes, the air stirs with the sound of the bell on Fife Street. She enjoys the din, a sound that fills the city and gives it an alertness, a sense of expectation. Nonceba looks to her left at City Hall. High on a pillar over its facade is the large wall clock; it reads quarter past two. She quickens her step, walks past the man selling watches and belts, who raises his arms at every passerby to display his watches. Past that. Past the Chips Corner, which releases a greasy smell of cooking oil and potatoes and vinegar. In front of City Hall with its gardens of peach roses grown en masse is the disused well, the first water source when the city was settled by the pioneer column. Today, only a bench remains affixed there, and a protective circular wall with an inscription on the edge of it. In front of the old well are the dozens and dozens of flower sellers, of all ages and apparel, mingling and haggling. Here, there is a spray of activity and a colorful array.

The flower sellers range from one side of the street—that is, from Ninth Avenue down the entire block of City Hall—on to the other side, at Selborne Avenue. It is a dazzling scene. Above the sellers, the flamboyant trees are in bloom; they cast a protective shade over the flowers, and a red and sizzling hue over the sellers. The petals are long, thin, multiple. It is a distinct panorama. The flowers are placed in buckets of water resting directly on the ground, at the feet of the sellers, whose voices rise like miniature bells into the petal-ridden air in order to welcome customers and identify each flower and declare its quality. "Fresh roses . . . flame lily . . . madam . . . flame lily very special flower . . . I give you bonus . . . madam . . ." Their voices clutch, flatter, cuddle, sweet-talk, and cajole. They bargain with the shoppers, exclaiming and then surrendering. A woman holds her hand tightly to her waist, arguing about a price, excited, shrill, then calming down. She laughs and turns her head away, moves from the customer and the blooms, and, using a small metal basin, sprinkles the petals with water. When it suits her, she looks up, and decides to change her mind, tightens her brow, leans forward, and lowers the price. Behind her, on Fife Street, the cars zoom past. Hooters blare. Cars skid, and miss, and move on. Drivers curse and slide with the traffic; they slow down at the intersection and roll down the windows impatiently. Pedestrians rush across the street and dart between cars at the Rixi taxi rank on the corner of Ninth and Fife. The woman finally exhales, accepts a bill, and surrenders a bunch of flowers. The sellers lower the price, then raise it for the next customer, then lower it even further than before. They breathe the fluorescent blooms, watchful. Red petals fall and cover the empty track within the pavement where the buyers linger; they walk over the fallen jacaranda blooms. It is a colorful exchange, the rows and rows of flowers of every tint and flourish, budding, falling, fully opened; pollen coats the tips of fingers held out. Each bunch of roses is wrapped in a piece of rippled cardboard, an elastic band wound tightly over it. The stems are cut at a slant so that the pores are not damaged and the flowers can breathe. Each seller has a metal bin full to capacity with flower stems, wilted blooms, discarded leaves, and crushed cardboard boxes. The sellers sit on the bins and press the flowers down, rest, and chat among themselves. Then they rise into the red flamboyant blooms and embrace the chrysanthemums.

Along Ninth Avenue, on the other side of City Hall, is the bus terminus catering to those going to the eastern suburbs: Four Winds, Kumalo, Iloana, Montrose, Southwold, Matsheumhlophe, Famona. The benches and sheds are full, lively with the repartee of conductors selling and punching tickets, the cry of orange sellers. The buses are lined up against the pavement, their engines droning. The women drag their children along. There are black girls recently enrolled in "A" schools, who wear neat blue uniforms from Montrose High and Eveline High; boys from Gifford High and Milton High; and toddlers from Thomas Aquinas, and Henry Low and Greenfield Primary. Across the way is Haddon and Sly, where you can buy silverware and the most expensive glass and chandeliers.

Nonceba avoids the crowds all around City Hall and remains on the opposite side of Fife Street; only when she has passed the next block does she cross over to the other side of the road, turning from Q.V. Pharmacy at the Kirrie Building, to O.K. Bazaars, past Woolworth's, over to Stella Nova Photo Studio, onward to Fifteenth Avenue and Wilson Street. Cars are parked facing the pavement and a man in a faded blue uniform is checking for expired meters and issuing tickets and sliding them under the wipers of each car. On the corner of this street are varieties of magazines and newspapers laid out on the ground—back copies of *Drum*, *Moto*, and *Parade*. The seller keeps his change in a hat turned upside down beside him. He has a mound of coins held in it. Nonceba greets the seller with a slight lift of her fingers. The magazine seller holds out a copy of *The Chronicle* to her. She shakes her head and opens the door at the corner of this street. She enters, steps quickly through. The door slides back and closes. The sound of the city is behind her. Ahead, a flight of steps, neatly polished. She walks slowly up the stairs to the second floor.

Nonceba stands in front of number 341 Kensington Flats. She unlocks the blue door and enters, turning on the light, then dimming it. The apartment has a parquet floor that spreads from the small corridor into the lounge, and there are two bedrooms facing each other, a bathroom, and a balcony. From the corridor, there is an arched entrance leading to the kitchen. Inside the kitchen are a small fridge, an electric kettle, pots and pans, a double sink, a stove. There are fitted cupboards; inside them are plates, more pans, and food. A pantry to the extreme left extends full height to the pine ceiling. Nonceba slips the package of fruit from her arm and places it in a basket near the sink. On her left is a small breakfast nook with a bench attached to the wall; two freestanding chairs with covers of red-and-white fabric face the wall. A broom closet is in one corner. She bends down to open the fridge door and takes out a bottle of Orange Crush. Then she gets a glass from the cupboard above her and carries it and the bottle into the lounge. She slides onto the three-seater couch and places her drink on a coaster in front of her on the coffee table. There is a small side table with a telephone on it. Two small windows look out onto a large square, where a rotating clothesline is positioned. She can look out at the balconies of the other apartments, which house potted plants and some outdoor chairs. During the weekends, the children play under the sheets, which have been put out to dry; garments are pinned all along the line. Often, one of the tenants shouts down from the top floor, telling the children to stop screaming. This increases their excitement, and they race through the clothing, pressing their faces into the drying white sheets; they are quiet, transformed into shadows. The sheets blow against their bodies, shaping them into smooth white stones. They wave their arms under the sheets and turn into giant birds too heavy for flight. The adults watch quietly from the balconies, regarding the children with amused impatience.

It has been a year since she moved to the city, and life has assumed an even pace for Nonceba. When she first arrived in Bulawayo, she went into the hospital several times for more surgery. With some powder on, she looks almost unharmed. Almost. At least no one stares. No one turns to look. No one asks questions.

Cephas has done exactly as he had stated he would do when he went to see her in Kezi. He gave her the bedroom across from his own. They live together. He deals with the hospital and arranges everything for her there; he enables her spirit. She finds strength through each of his unexpected gestures. They live in each other's solitude. In a way, they live separately.

In her room, there is a small single bed, a wardrobe, and a radio, but no mirror. Nonceba has added other touches of her own—like the picture on one wall, something she impulsively tore out of a magazine, showing a field of yellow daisies. Cephas placed the picture carefully in a frame for her. They hammered a nail into the wall. He asked her how high she wanted the picture. She picked a spot and kept her finger there till Cephas was standing beside her. He marked the spot with a pencil. After the painting was raised, they both stood back and looked at it. "Perfect," she said, straightening the picture a little. This room is now completely hers. She has a small round table, where she throws some of her things when she comes home, a catchall for a book, a magazine, a pen. She likes the soft yellow bedspread with its frilled edges.

A window looks out to the busy street below. Pigeons perch on the roof of the building opposite. She can see into the offices across the road. On the edge of the building, a flag beats against the air. It is darkened by the smoke from the cars; torn, flapping in the wind. A flag for a new nation. Nonceba watches the street in all its changing moods. At this stage, she knows by sight the people who work in the buildings across from her window. She sees them walk in, walk out, stand on the steps. The pigeons flap . . . flap . . . and fly away. They cry out, dirty the ledge, swoop between buildings, and disappear from her view. She can hear them beyond the window. They sit in every nook under the eaves, tapping on the roof of Kensington Flats.

Cephas has provided her with a home, and a new life. She has no regrets in coming to the city. Certainly their relationship is undefined. It is pleasurable, supportive. They both avoid defining it, embraced by an innocence born of the tragic circumstances of their unity. They do not complicate it with questions they dare not answer. Around 5:30 every evening, the traffic in the city becomes a murmur; by 6:30 it hums. Then the streets are empty—so empty, you can hear the soft sound of tires as a bicycle goes by. When Nonceba again looks through the window, the noiselessness is visible. Dim footsteps. Streetlights. A lone vehicle waiting for the light to change—red, green, amber. Cephas returns home soon after. They do not discuss their relationship, the limits of it. They focus on the things that need to be done, the things they are definite about. Helping: a type of rescue. He helps her. They avoid the most imprecise element, love, the least predictable, the most enduring human quality, the most intriguing, the most difficult to control. They let their feelings exist separate from each task, from their tremors.

Nonceba is grateful to Cephas, thankful for the existence of his type of gentleness, which allows an imprecise distance. She does not know if she has helped him. She would like to have helped him, somehow. He is no longer a stranger—it has been twelve months—yet in this matter, he is unknown to her. Being here with him is as close as she has been to any man: intimate. She carries visible scars; he shields her from the invisible ones. Sometimes when she looks at him, she sees his hesitation, his absolute hurt. The same hurt she had seen in his eyes when they met. It is still there, like a quiet flame, not forgotten. She has no idea what to say to him in order to banish that hurt. She has her journey. The nature of their friendship is in the elimination of detail, of the specific, in order to free her. They cannot yet discuss matters that concern the cause of their despair. Not yet. Not together. Such thoughts remain separate, lingering in the corners of their minds when they say something to each other about dinner, or about whether the light in the passage should be left on or not, or about the day's purchases. Their thoughts are completely absorbed by the full weight of the past. The mind is buried in its own despair, but they survive, day to day, in their friendship. The past for them is so much heavier than the present; it exists with an absolute claim. To sip some tea, to pass the sugar, their fingers meet: memory. A delicate act of forgiveness; to be alive at all seems a betrayal. They should have saved her, even by their will alone. This is their preoccupation, and they acknowledge it, and live within it, somehow.

She has bought large yellow roses from the flower sellers at City Hall. She places them in a glass vase, which she puts on the telephone table. She adds salt to the tepid water. In a day, they will open, and the room will carry a fresh smell of roses, a pleasant scent. She likes the yellow roses most, and sometimes she mixes them with white ones. If she changes the water regularly, the flowers will last longer than a week. She stands a long time looking at the flowers. This sort of flower could never grow on Kwakhe sands. She is amused. A detail like this tells how far she is from Kezi.

"I have found a job," Nonceba says.

"Yes, I have managed to find a job for you. I have been waiting to tell you, until we were sitting down. I wanted to surprise you. How did you know?"

"You have also found me something?" she asks.

"I have. A job in the library. Would you like it?"

"I have to think it over. Tell me more about it. I like the job I have found, though. I met the people there. They seemed nice, welcoming. I like the hours, too," she says.

"I thought you would like something to do with books. The public library needs someone. It sounds interesting."

"Hmm. I must think . . . "

"You will have to decide for yourself about taking the job or not. But they would like to know tomorrow. I said I knew someone. I was there all morning doing some research. I know the chief librarian, Mr. Drake, very well. He is a kind man. You might enjoy working with him. He is very caring about the library, every aspect of it. He is seeking to improve it. The number of users has more than doubled since independence. He needs a hand."

"I would like to meet him. Two jobs. It is all good news, in any case."

"You will consider it?"

"I will. Can I let you know my decision in the morning? I would like to think some more about the whole matter. It is so sudden."

"We still must celebrate. Imagine finding a job for you on the same day that you have found one for yourself. It is remarkable," he says.

He swings from the stove, where he is preparing a meal, and faces her. He does not embrace her. He avoids touch. Too threatening. Especially for her. She is not ready.

"I have found a job. On my own. In the street. I have found a job for myself. I feel happy about it!" she tells him with delight. Her first triumph. It is important. Though she has said she will let him know in the morning, it is basically decided. It is clear that she would rather take the job she has secured. He agrees with her choice. He must let her find places to inhabit without his help.

"Duly's?" Cephas asks, surprised. How does one find a job at a place with a name like that? he wonders. Quaint.

"Yes. Duly's. On Wilson Street." She lets herself fall onto the couch. Exhausted by joy. Happy. Free. A new path has opened for her; she will meet other people at work, build new friendships, have colleagues, discover qualities of her own. She has the strength for it, the resolve. His mind travels. Hers is satisfied.

Nonceba throws the folded newspaper at him playfully. She is going to keep the newspaper with the advert she had circled and responded to, a task accomplished, a test passed. To have gone through the interview so easily, to have succeeded; there are not many people with a good high school certificate in the city. She has an advantage. Education for everyone is being constantly interrupted by the war. Schools close down. They remain closed. Especially the mission schools located in rural areas.

Nonceba has an astounding capacity for joy, he thinks. Small, thin, agile. She wears plain clothes, small skirts, white blouses; pale colors wrap over her frame. To him, not unattractive; to another man, perhaps too concealing. A subterfuge, a modest wardrobe, unassuming, like her own nature. When she laughs, he remembers the depth of her hurt; his hurt. When she is as happy as now, he imagines her terror; his pain. On her face are the lingering scars; his capacity for love. Her laughter echoes in him.

He, too, has nightmares. In the night, he is drowning in blood. He is swallowing, drowning. He wakes in a sweat. He has already walked to her door and touched her feet to see if she is there, to find out if she, too, is as desperate as he is. He stands still, shocked at his own subconscious action, at his loneliness. He peels his hand off her, cautious. He walks slowly back to his room, silent, afraid he has already woken her. His heart is beating heavily. Is it fear? Is it love? Often he would like to enter her room with her permission, her knowledge, and sleep on the floor beside her bed, to roll himself there, a presence. He would shelter her, shelter in her dreams. He would be rid of his own dreams. He returns to his bed, turns over, and sinks into an interminable darkness. He is struggling out of that darkness, out of breath. When he opens his eyes, there is no darkness, no light. He is lying still in his bed. An arm on his forehead. Blood.

Her movements and speech are unhurried. Nonceba keeps her hair plaited in neat, straight rows, beautiful and precise. He is drawn to her by much more than what is immaculate, orderly, perfectly formed: the beauty of her presence. Nonceba has grown on him like a good song, Cephas thinks. Thenjiwe made him want to seize all of time in his arms and make it theirs.

Sisters, two sides, but not quite opposite: connected. Their birth, and a life shared, linked. The trace of one voice is in the other, the gesture of one reflected in the other, the easy joy, the shape of a nail, of a bone, especially the voice: oneness. They exist each in the other, and where one life ended, so did the other. He knows that what he sees of Nonceba is only what is recoverable; he has made her whole for himself. It would be too much to ask her to be entire. It would be impossible. It is enough that she can laugh with him. Thenjiwe made him abandon himself to her, and he knew what it was to exist completely in the realm of another human being, to be as close to her as skin. Nonceba makes him steady. She offers nothing that throws him off balance, nothing of the sort, and regards him without extreme passion, from a far distance really, perhaps even with some disbelief. Of course, she has no reason to offer more than her presence; she keeps him aloof, like a brother, yet has become all that is dear to him.

Thenjiwe offered him everything: in one afternoon, his life changed completely, as though he had never before lived, never seen sunset or dawn or the shadows at noon. A woman turned and gave him her name like an embrace. He abandoned everything and wanted only the light in Thenjiwe's eyes. When they considered the future, too much seemed to have already been consumed. That was her attraction—the ability for risk; her total absorption in a single moment, as though all of time were a distraction; her insatiable interest in him, even beyond what he understood or could reveal of himself. He loved her for her intensity, her capacity for surprise. He misses Thenjiwe and the profound love they had found. He misses her. He is not transferring emotions, certainly; there is something new in his current state. New, unknown, recently discovered. He is sure of it. He wonders if perhaps there are different kinds of love possible between a man and a woman, as there are different lives, lived: different melodies to the single theme of love.

Nonceba is here, with him; this, surely, is trust. She trusts him. He dares not compare them, the living and the dead. He dares not choose. He need not choose, nor even imagine what sort of love he prefers; the image of one is safely in the other. He dares not question his continuity of emotion, of love—a form of incest, loving two sisters. In this case, only a defiance of death, perhaps. No. Certainly not incest. It is more accurate to consider it a kinship of desire. That is where his incest lies, in desiring the same flesh, the same voice, the same nakedness. This is his form of guilt, his type of sin. He approves his own permanent passion, his sentiment—desire that survives, intact, beyond death. He wonders if he is callous, selfish, in his attitude, given the circumstances. He wonders if one can be said to be callous, indifferent, in the matters of love and affection when one is so thoroughly involved. An irony, to be said to be unfeeling when one feels so much. Given Thenjiwe's death. Given that Nonceba witnessed that death. Herself terribly harmed. Given that he truly loved Thenjiwe. Given all this, how has he allowed himself to feel something new? Is this a love born of hurt, of despair, in a terrain of tragedy and disbelief? Is it a kind of salve, an emotion to heal his fractured being? And if so, is it enough? Can it contain and sustain him?

Is love an emotion someone can control, suppress, or is it an instant act of recognition? First your vision is empty; then the day seems suddenly short, the time apart intolerable, night too long and filled with that endless loneliness in the mind—waiting. He wonders at his degree of desecration. He is still innocent, to a point; he has let Nonceba decide both their lives. A year has passed and they have lived together. He can wait. Each morning, he wakes to Thenjiwe's presence; to her absolute absence. Must he feel guilt, as he does? Must his love feel like failure, a house collapsed? A transgression of sorts. He feels the lack of a certain integrity, the sort of stamina that engenders virtues like abstinence, a restraint in the heart. He wonders if he has exceeded his own economy; a man attempting to live beyond his means. There is too much for him to juggle. He is an unskilled and blind juggler who has to imagine not only the shape of his objects but also their number, distance, and their flight from his own hands.

Nonceba has grown on him, that is all, like a good song. He wants to help, to sustain, not to contain. He wants her not to doubt her own freedom, to know his distance from her. He knows her frailty. If she decides to move out of the flat, he will help her find another. He will even give her up; this, his final disguise. He will stand by and witness her life move on without him. She has already helped him. To watch her happiness unfold is to know that he has already helped; they have each dealt with the past. It is not only that he wants to help; there is grief. He is grieving. Nonceba eases him, makes him feel pardon from that irreversible death. Perhaps if he had stayed in Kezi . . . What then? Would Thenjiwe have died in his company, as well? Was she not an easy target because he was not there, two women on their own in a forlorn place like Kezi in the middle of a war such as this? Two women. The soldiers armed, burning villages, intimidating the land with torture, death, and their might? The soldiers in a ceremony of their own.

The love of a dead sister; the love of a living sister. The love of both. He feels himself located between them, suspended, unable to pronounce love of one of them, the living sister, the one who can cure him of his dreams; he need not abandon his yearning for Thenjiwe. It is too familiar, too near. He has nurtured it since that uncertain year of 1979, when they were both waiting for freedom to find them—indeed, when the entire country was waiting for freedom—and they found each other instead. Then independence arrived and brought with it a spectacular arena for a different war, in which they were all casualties. And she, Thenjiwe, among its first victims. And Nonceba, who at least has lived. He had watched the city change during that year, and he moved to the flat from Mpopoma Township, partly to prove to himself that independence had really come, to share in its immense promise, in its cityscape. He could never have imagined Thenjiwe living in the middle of this city with him, the center of her pulse being Kezi. He had not even considered it till her name leapt from the pages of the newspaper and his arms trembled with a sorrow he could not curtail. First, he had disbelieved every word. Then he had wept, trusting every word.

He is waiting for a sign from Nonceba. Not the charmed movement of her arm, which engages his mind as he watches her hands disappear under the cushion as she rests on the couch, or when, her elbow bent toward him, she pulls the strap of her sundress back over her shoulder, unaware that he is staring, immobile. He would like to keep such moments, prolong them, return over and again to them, Nonceba the gentle wind in the center of his dream. He condemns himself for noticing her in this manner; for his need to possess each movement of her arm. He does not press her, however. He is waiting for the certainty of her words. He wants to be sure. He can only wait for Nonceba to notice him as completely as he has imagined her. Desire cannot be contained. It reaches out, unsanctioned, willing to be expressed. The more it is doubted, censored, contained, the tenderer it grows, the more effusive; then it overwhelms its source. It tarnishes nothing. The purest moment is when desire is not requited; when it is only an expectation, a belief, a quiet emotion. Desire is like hunger. It attacks the body and makes it bend. His begins with a hurt so enormous, he cannot contain it. He has to find its source. He links the hurt to the absence of its source, to Thenjiwe, but for them, it is too late.

He will wait till Nonceba turns to him with a wonder to match his own, with an equal wish, till she, too, feels that if he leaves the room, her world will diminish. If he holds her, Thenjiwe will be in his arms, too. Could he survive that? And what about Nonceba? Would his presence then feel like safety or a threat?

Nonceba removes her sandals and rests her feet on the stool beside the table. Another day. The door opens. Cephas. She looks up at him. She rises and helps him place his folders and books on the table. He removes his spectacles, places them on the table. Broken glass.

"Oh . . . your glasses . . . Did you drop them?" she asks, alarmed.

"They fell just outside as I was coming up the stairs. They were in my shirt pocket."

She moves her fingers over the crack. The surface is still even. He picks the glasses up, puts them on. Light refracts, falls on the opposite wall. He replaces them on the table, defeated.

"I will have them replaced tomorrow. I need them for my reading; otherwise, I will become slow with my research. I am already behind."

She examines the glasses closely. She puts them in their black case. The frame is intact. Secure.

"When I was a child, I feared finding a perfect hiding place, one in which I would never be found. I imagined being alone, undiscovered, lost. I did not even pause to think that all I would need to do would be to walk out of my hiding place if no one were to find me."

She is happy. She teases him. Is it possible she is saying that he has found her? That she can never be alone after this? Is she speaking of her own growing independence? It is the first time she has spoken of her childhood.

"So. What did you file today?" she asks after he has removed his jacket and put it in his room. He is about to sit down next to her, to ask her how she is finding her new work, if she will remain there. She often refers to his explanation of a year ago, of finding her name and that of her sister, Thenjiwe, in a newspaper. He does not answer. He could bring the paper home, but that would depress her. He knows it is her way of dealing with the incident, with the death of her sister, of skirting the subject, of not focusing on the worst aspects of the event, yet not avoiding the subject completely. This is her way of being brave; they both understand that. She does not talk about Thenjiwe. Not once since leaving Kezi. He does not answer her question regarding the files. He only turns and smiles at her. Her strength often amazes him. They have become friends.

He works for the archives of the National Museums and Monuments of Zimbabwe. He had no business cutting out that particular notice in the newspaper, or filing it away, as he stated to her then. They both know this. He should have simply told her that he had been reading the paper like anybody else. He must have sounded very suspicious to her, a year ago, to link his discovery of her and her sister to his work. His discovery sounded official. He had felt awkward, appearing so suddenly in her life, making proposals that sounded absurd even to him. Two strangers caught in the most difficult situation, sharing the same loss. He had no prepared words and carried only the force of his impulse. His conviction. An incredible and lingering love. The words would come with the moment of their meeting. He had hoped that she already knew about him from her sister.

Knowing Nonceba better, he now understands Thenjiwe. Such a circuitous route to discover her, he thinks, to know her, to have better cared for her, and, as he wishes desperately now, to have protected her. How could he not have heard the pleading behind her every word, from each motion of her body, as he held her, from bone to bone? How had he missed her nuance as close as he was to her, as involved, missed her tears, when he remembered almost everything about her, each word she uttered, each of his own words to her?

Thenjiwe needed other kinds of truths before accepting their own truth. They hardly knew each other. He had not known how to handle that sort of desperate emotion in him. She had hesitated; he had hesitated, and left. He had not heard her at all. Perhaps this was the similarity between the sisters, to ask him to wait, till she again calls his name. He would let Nonceba be. Leave her and bury his own longing, but he would not walk away. When he met Nonceba, then, he was seeking penance, for an absence, for a forgetfulness, for abandon: He now felt it was he who had walked away. Thenjiwe had asked him to stay. He needs to sustain the attitude of the penitent: a contrite heart, which dares not double its original sin. He is beginning to mistake his weakness for fortitude.

He needs a sterile solution to wash wounds; an ointment to wash both their wounds. He is an amalgam, man and martyr. No. It is not much to sacrifice love; he does not deserve the term at all. He is not a martyr. He has nothing to surrender. What has he got to sacrifice? If he turns to look, whose life has he saved? He remembers collecting Nonceba from the hospital after she has been discharged for the last time from the surgery, then, later, sitting down and unwinding the bandage from her face. The bandage is light, spoiled; it peels off like a protecting net. He closes his eyes to remove the last layer, which clings to the skin. She has endured the worst. He replaces the dressing, carefully following the instructions the nurse has provided him with. He says nothing. His movements alone fill the room; his arm stirs around her head, swinging, slowly folding her into his armpit, following the bandage. Closely, he searches her eyebrows, her cheeks, her stillness. If there is to be pain, he must be the one to bear it.

She offers to cook. He remains seated and listens to her movements in the next room. He pulls her hospital card from a yellow folder. There is a staccato narration: ". . . inflicted as by a sharp object . . . could be a blade . . . victim did not see the instrument . . . grievous harm . . . lips cut off . . . urgent surgery required . . . skin graft." He replaces the card in the folder and moves to the kitchen. He already guesses that she will not eat. Perhaps she will drink something. He discovers that it is weeks before she has any appetite.

He must retreat from Nonceba; perhaps he has become too involved in replicating histories. He should stick to restorations of ancient kingdoms, circular structures, beehive huts, stone knives, broken pottery, herringbone walls, the vanished pillars in an old world. A new nation needs to restore the past. His focus, the beehive hut, to be installed at Lobengula's ancient kraal, kwoBulawayo, the following year. His task is to learn to re-create the manner in which the tenderest branches bend, meet, and dry, the way grass folds smoothly over this frame and weaves a nest, the way it protects the cool, livable places within—deliverance.